In Cassie's Corner

by
Dale Mayer

IN CASSIE'S CORNER
Dale Mayer
Valley Publishing
Copyright © 2011

ISBN: 0987741179
ISBN-13: 978-0-9877411-7-2

DEDICATION

This book is dedicated to my daughter Kara. It's the first YA book I wrote for her and is one that touches my heart the most. Enjoy!

ACKNOWLEDGMENTS

IN CASSIE'S CORNER wouldn't have been possible without the support of my friends and family. Many hands helped with proofreading, editing, and beta reading to make this book come together. Special thanks to my editor Pat Thomas. I had a vision, but it took many people to make that vision real.

I thank you all

CHAPTER ONE

Moonlight and shadows danced through sixteen-year-old Cassie Merchant's mind as she slumbered, not quite asleep and not quite awake, caught in the mysterious world in-between.

"Cassie. Cassie."

The whispers, so soft, so gentle, made her smile. She snuggled deeper under her duvet.

The whisper came again. "Cassie."

She stilled, recognizing the voice. Right person; wrong place.

She bolted upright, her blankets falling around her waist. Shadows made it hard to see. The lights on her purple iPod showed two in the morning. She blinked then gasped at the figure sitting on the windowsill.

Inside her room.

"Todd? What are you doing here?"

His same sassy grin gleamed in the darkness.

"Dad will kill me if he finds you here." She shifted the blankets out of her way to shuffle back up against her padded headboard. Glancing down, she realized the shoulder of her sleep shirt had slipped down. Heat climbed her cheeks. She yanked the offending material back into place and hauled her blankets up to her neck. Thank heavens for the gloomy light. "What are you doing here?" At the sight of her open window behind him, she added, "And how did you get in?"

Todd, his hair falling every which way, smirked. "How do you think I got in?"

"I have no idea." She tucked her shoulder-length hair behind her ears. "Why are you here? You know how much trouble I will be in if my parents find out you're here, right?"

"I know. I'm sorry, but it'll be all right. I promise."

Cassie snorted. "Right. Like you promised to help me with my science project last week? Or how about your promise to show up for my debate? Remember how *that* turned out?"

"Are you still on about that? I said I was sorry."

His devilish grin tore her heart out. Heartthrob Todd. The name had stuck after Penny's mom coined the term. And it wasn't just that his jet black hair curled in such a way that all the girls wanted to twine it around their fingers. Or the way that grin of his slid sideways, catching everyone's breath. Nor was it only about his lean, six-foot frame that moved so strongly and easily through life. No, it had more to do with him being a good boy wrapped up in bad boy packaging.

All the girls adored him.

Good thing Cassie was immune. On the other hand, his brother, with the same adorable curls, matching lopsided grin and warm, melted chocolate eyes…Oh, boy.

"Yeah, right. Whatever." Cassie studied Todd. For all his bravado, she'd never seen him look so pale. His stark white skin shone in the darkness. He'd have made a great vampire. And he stayed up all hours of the night. But that went along with being eighteen and almost done with school. Cassie, however, needed her sleep, otherwise…

No. Todd looked upset, sad. Or maybe lost was the better word. She couldn't really pin it down, but whatever was bothering him, now bothered her. Todd always knew what to do in life. He never had doubts or qualms about his actions.

Cassie yawned. "Okay. What's going on?"

Todd didn't do heart-to-hearts well. It took him awhile, but he did get around to explaining, eventually.

"I can't tell you all of it. But you will hear some stuff about me that's wrong. Very wrong. Stuff I don't know how to put right. I need your help, Cassie. I've never asked you for anything before; well okay, maybe I have, but this time, I'm begging. Please, don't believe what you hear and don't think bad of me. I didn't do what they say I did."

"They? Who are they?"

He turned his head away. She heard an odd sound.

A sniffle? For the first time, Cassie started to panic. "Todd," she whispered, her voice hoarse with worry. "What are you talking about?"

"I can't explain." His voice cracked. "Besides, you'll find out soon enough."

Somewhere in the house a door slammed and voices rose. Todd straightened to stare at Cassie's bedroom door. A sliver of light flashed at the bottom of her door. Muted voices sounded.

Cassie caught her breath, squeezed her eyes shut, and slid down under the covers. If they got caught…

Her mother's hushed voice droned outside the door; her father's harsher one interrupted constantly. Cassie couldn't make out what they were saying. Then she heard stomping footsteps that faded away, as if her parents had headed downstairs. A minute later, the hallway light went out. Cassie's room returned to total darkness.

She released the pent up breath she hadn't been aware she held and turned to face Todd again.

Only he wasn't there.

Cassie bolted out of bed, whispering sharply, "Todd? Where are you?"

His voice, thin and distant, answered, "I'll be back. Remember what I said."

She raced to the open window to search the darkness outside.

Passing clouds hid the moon and the shadows hid Todd's tracks. He'd disappeared. Too many trees and houses kept her from seeing what direction he'd gone – if he'd gone. Her gaze swept the room but there was no place he could have hidden.

Her closet door was open, the interior jammed full. Knowing the idea was ridiculous, she bent and looked under her bed anyway. A balled up sock nestled amongst the dust bunnies. Yuck.

He had to have gone out the window.

She rushed back to the window to study the height from the ground. Except...how? Then Todd was a street jumper and pulled off some pretty wicked stunts. She should have asked him more questions. Next time.

He'd sounded so sad. It freaked her out.

She hoped he wouldn't do anything stupid. But what if he already had? Maybe the better question was – what did other people *think* he'd done?

Disturbed, Cassie crawled back into her bed, pulling the covers up high. It was the end of May and balmy for this time of year, but the cozy comfort of her own bed no longer felt welcoming or warm.

Sleep was slow coming.

Her best friend was in trouble.

***

Morning had never been Cassie's best time of day. Today wouldn't be so bad, except it was Saturday and that meant housework. It also meant she'd get the afternoon off to head to a movie with her friends or even just hang at the park. A good thing, because Saturdays with nothing to do, sucked.

Cassie studied her reflection in her bedroom mirror. Those *were* bags under her eyes. She'd always wondered what that term meant, and now she knew. Nuts. She'd hardly slept after Todd's visit, then, after she'd finally fallen into a deep sleep, her mom had awakened her early. Not a good start.

Throwing on jeans and a tank top, she swept her flyaway hair up in a ponytail and headed downstairs.

Her parents sat in the kitchen. The matched set as she called them. Perfect with each other and no room for anyone else. Because of it her childhood had often felt cold and lonely. Their conversation stopped as she walked in. She gave them a cursory glance and headed for the coffee pot. Her friends had turned her onto coffee months ago, much to her parent's disapproval.

"Hi, honey. Did you have a good night?"

Cassie slid a sidelong glance at her mother. Was it her imagination, or did she have her I'm-determined-to-not-let-Cassie-know-something's-wrong look.

"I guess," she murmured, her fingers crossed. White lies were allowable in her book. She filled her cup and added cream before turning around. Her parents stared at each other. Her mother tilted her head in Cassie's direction, and her father frowned.

Great. Charades.

"So what's the matter?" Cassie lifted her cup higher, letting the steam bathe her tired face.

Her mother jumped into the silence. "What makes you think there's something the matter, honey?"

Cassie rolled her eyes. "Mom, you're telling Dad to talk to me, and he's frowning because he doesn't want to. Right?"

Her father threw the newspaper down, disgust washing across his face. "Oh for the love of...Abby, just tell her."

Her mother got up, smoothed down her skirt then walked to where Cassie slouched against the kitchen sink. "Cassie, we have bad news." She pulled Cassie's cup out of her hand and set it on the counter.

Cassie's heart pounded, her empty hands clenched. The last time her mom had acted this way, Grams had died. Her stomach twisted. That had been horrible. Grams had understood Cassie. She'd always had time for her. Three years later, Cassie still missed her. She wiped her hands on her jeans. "What happened?"

Abby glanced at Cassie's father.

"Stop it, Mom. Just come out and tell me." Cassie twisted sideways, snagged her coffee cup up again and took a sip. It wasn't much, but it did provide a slight barrier against what was coming.

"Your father spoke to Adam Spence."

Cassie closed her eyes, her shoulders sagging. Oh no. Any contact with Todd's alcoholic father came under the heading of bad news. Maybe this would explain Todd's cryptic statements last night.

The words blurted out of Abby's mouth. "Todd's dead. He was killed in a car accident last night."

Cassie's eyes flew open, and she straightened abruptly. "What? No, that's not possible." She swayed, her coffee washing high up the sides of the cup.

Abby pulled the cup from Cassie's frozen fingers and led her to the closest kitchen chair, pushing her to sit. Her mother had to be wrong. Todd dead? Not possible. "There has to be some mistake," she whispered.

Her father jumped in, his voice harsh and condemning. "There isn't. He was drinking and driving and managed to kill himself. A chip off the old block. I told you that boy was trouble. And isn't it a damn good thing you weren't in the vehicle with him?"

She glared at her father as his words filtered into her dazed mind. "Todd doesn't…didn't drink." Cassie didn't understand. How could this be? This had to be a mistake.

"Cassie, honey?"

Her mother hovered at her side. Cassie looked up. "I'm okay, Mom. Just confused." *And horrified.* "I can't believe he's dead. Todd was so full of life. He was fun to be with."

"Too much fun, if you ask me. The only thing that boy was heading for was trouble. Well, he found it." Her father grabbed up his newspaper, opened it and held it between him and his family.

"Victor. That's no way to speak about the dead." Her mother frowned at the paper he seemed determined to read.

It rustled loudly before he lowered the pages to glare at Abby and Cassie. "Just because he's dead doesn't change his actions. He drank, then he got behind the wheel of a car and drove off the road. He killed himself. Thank God he didn't drag anyone else over that cliff with him."

Cassie shook her head, trying to comprehend the nightmare suffocating her. "I know you never liked him, Dad. But he wasn't like that. He was always very careful with me."

"That's because he wanted inside your—"

"Victor." Abby snapped. "That's enough. Give Cassie some time. He was her friend."

"Humph." The paper lifted and her dad retreated into a wall of silence.

How could something so major change – and yet her world still looked so much the same? Blinking to hold back tears, she realized there had to be a mistake. It just wasn't possible. "Something's wrong," she muttered under her breath. "I saw him just last night."

Her father lowered the paper. His deadly quiet voice stabbed into the silence. "What did you just say?"

Surely she hadn't spoken aloud? Oh God. Her world was collapsing and her father would be out for blood. She gave a broken laugh. Like that mattered now.

Ignoring him, Abby pulled a kitchen chair close and sat down. "Did you say you saw him last night?" She leaned forward. "When?"

"Last night. I woke up…" She shook her head, rubbing her temple as she tried to sort through her suddenly rocked world. "And he was there. In my room."

Her father's fist crashed to the table.

"What?" he roared. "That boy was in your bedroom?"

"It's not like I invited him or anything. He just showed up." Cassie rolled her eyes. Her dad was so-o-o protective. If it weren't so irritating, it would be cute.

Victor beetled his thick bushy brows together. He opened his mouth to speak again, but Abby held her hand up, stopping him. Confusion twisted her pretty features. "Please, Cassie. You need to explain."

Her mom wouldn't be able to hold her dad off for long. Cassie rushed to explain. "Someone called my name and woke me up around two in the morning. When I rolled over, Todd stood by my window. We talked until the hall lights came on and we heard you two talking outside my door. I hushed him up. When everything went quiet and dark again, I called out to him, but he'd gone."

Victor opened his mouth then closed it again. He looked dumbfounded and exchanged a blank look with Abby before he shrugged his shoulders and returned to reading. Abby slumped back into her chair, her gaze jumping from Victor to Cassie then back again.

Cassie could see they weren't pleased – but they weren't yelling, so that had to be a good thing. Maybe she'd escape without punishment after all.

Her voice as gentle as a buttercup, Abby reached a hand to cover hers. "Cassie, Todd died just after eleven last night. At two in the morning his body was already in the morgue."

CHAPTER TWO

Cassie worked like a robot throughout the morning, vacuuming, cleaning, dusting. Mindless stuff that occupied her hands while emotions and questions spun endlessly inside. The well-meaning looks from her parents were easy to ignore. She'd *never* be able to talk to them. Not about Todd's supposed death, or his appearance in her room last night. She wanted to blame them. Strike out at them. Fairness or logic didn't factor in this. Her best friend had died.

The first tears fell without warning. Once they started, she couldn't hold them back. With a cleaning cloth in one hand and a bottle of cleaning spray in the other, Cassie rested her forehead against the big bay window in the living room and bawled.

"Oh sweetheart." Cassie dimly heard her mother's gentle voice, as someone took the rag and container from her hands and pulled the rubber gloves off. Her mother wrapped her in a caring hug. Darned if it didn't make Cassie feel better. She'd never been able to get close to her mom the way her best friends Suzie and Penny were with their moms. They told theirs everything.

Cassie would have liked to, but the words never came out right. Or they weren't received right. She didn't know.

She hiccupped and pulled back slightly.

"I'm sorry, honey. I know he was your friend." Abby patted her back.

"My best friend, Mom." She just didn't get it. Todd *was* special. How could he be gone? The world would be such a dark place without him.

"I'm going out for a while." Cassie raced to her room. From the door she walked to the spot where she'd seen Todd standing. Surely, there'd be some proof he'd been there. She checked the carpet and the windowsill, searching for a speck of dirt, a shoe imprint, something. There was nothing.

She couldn't stand being inside a moment longer. She ran to her bathroom and washed her face then returned to her bedroom to grab a hoodie. Taking the stairs two at a time, she was out the door in seconds.

Ignoring the world around her, she headed to the park that had been their special place. It would be full of moms and toddlers at this hour, but she knew an area where she could be alone. Her cell phone rang. She checked the caller ID as she walked. Penny. She stuffed the phone back in her pocket, unanswered. She just couldn't talk about this yet.

At the park, she hiked to the far corner where the original rusty swing set still stood beside the large almost empty sandbox. She'd spent many happy hours here with Todd. Over the years they'd covered almost every topic. Older by two years and with a difficult father, Todd had been a great listener through the rough patches growing up. He had understood so much.

Where was he now when she needed him?

The sense of letdown, of being abandoned, was stupid. Todd hadn't left her – he'd died. He hadn't done it on purpose. He wouldn't. She knew that, but knowing it didn't stop the wave of anger at his absence. Selfish. Stupid. But it had been the same after Grams died.

Cassie sat on the cracked rubber swing seat, drifting back and forth, the steady creaking of the rusted chain comforting in its constancy. The area was deserted – just the way she liked it.

Todd used to pick up coffee, then text her to get her butt over here in five minutes or he'd drink both cups. She smiled through her tears, murmuring, "I should have bought one in his honor."

"Thanks for the thought."

Who said that? Cassie frowned. "I must be losing it."

"Scaredy cat."

The humorous yet so familiar whisper made Cassie drag her feet on the ground, bringing the swing to a halt. Ever so slowly, afraid to hope, she turned around and watched Todd walk toward her.

"Todd?" His name slipped out on a shocked breath. She let out a whoop and raced toward him. Her heart swelled. She knew everyone had been wrong. She bounced with joy. "They said you were dead!"

His lips formed a sad smile that made her heart cry. He looked so lost. She reached out to touch him. But touch what? She could almost see through him – his features, his clothes – so substantial yet flimsy. Her hand dropped. She blinked several times.

"Oh my God! Todd? Are you...a ghost?" She gasped, her eyes opening wide.

"I am." His eye lit with sardonic humor. Trust him to get a kick out of the situation.

Cassie gaped like a child seeing Santa Claus for the first time.

"What? How?"

"I know. Weird, huh?"

She shook her head. "No. Weird is eating onion and jam sandwiches or liking punk rock. This is freaky shit."

He grinned. "Trust you to put it in perspective." He moved a few steps closer.

A breeze picked up around them. Cassie shivered, wrapping her arms around her tightly. She cast a quick glance around the surrounding area. Were there other ghosts here, too? Or was Todd alone? An oddity?

Zipping her gaze back to Todd, relief washed through her. "I was afraid you'd disappear when I looked away, - like you did last night."

"And I might. I'm not real good at this yet." His smile, so like when he'd been alive, now lacked his special glow.

"It's something you can control? What's it like?" It's not what she'd meant to ask, but the question had jumped out. She backed up to her swing and sat, her eyes glued on him as she waited for his answers.

"It's not much fun." He shimmered in front of her. "I'm lonely but not alone. I found others like me."

"Like you?" she asked cautiously. "As in dead?"

He laughed. That same warm chuckle that had always made her feel special, as if he'd really listened and liked what she said, who she was. "Kinda. Not sure dead is dead, now that I'm here. If you know what I mean."

Not sure she did, but she assumed he did. "Is this what you meant last night about things that I'll hear and not to believe them? To hear that you're dead, only you really aren't?"

His humor winked out. "No. I'm definitely dead."

She frowned, not ready to accept that. "What happened? They say you were drinking and driving. Were you?"

"No!" He grimaced and glanced away.

Afraid he didn't want her to know the truth, Cassie pressed forward. "Are you sure? You know you can tell me anything, right?"

The muscle in his jaw worked. Finally he closed his eyes, raising his face to the sun as if basking in its warmth. "Cassie, you know I don't drink and drive. I was in that car, yes. But *if* I was drinking, I was *not* driving."

Puzzled, Cassie studied his face. The rays pierced his form like arrows before landing in the grass behind. Yet he cast no shadow.

He pivoted, his green eyes glinting as the light hit them. "You know how I feel about that."

She nodded. His father had gotten caught drunk driving after he'd hit an old lady crossing the road. The woman had survived, but Todd's dad had lost his license for a while. He'd gotten off with only a few months of jail time, served on weekends, and community service for his first offense. Todd hated what his father had done. He'd sworn he would never drink and drive himself.

Cassie believed him. "If? I don't understand. Don't you remember?"

The corners of his mouth turned down as puzzlement filled his eyes. "I don't know." When she started to speak, he jumped in again, his hands out, imploring. "I know that sounds like a cop-out. But I really don't remember. Maybe it's because I'm dead. Or maybe I was drunk, asleep in the car. I don't know!" He ran his fingers through his curls, almost pulling on them. "It's driving me crazy, Cassie. I don't know who was driving or why I'd have let them behind the wheel of my car."

She studied his face. His last words had that tiny bit of doubt falling away. Todd never let anyone drive his car – ever. "So someone else drove last night. That's easy. Do you remember who you were with? What you were doing?"

He shook his head.

"Let's start with the last thing you *do* remember."

"I remember a party at Rob's house. Low key, normal – yet fun. We played that new game I told you about, on our laptops."

Cassie rolled her eyes. "Right. *That* new game. Like there isn't a new one every month. How long did you play?"

"Around eleven, maybe a bit later. Rob's dad came home about a half hour before and told us to start packing it in. Rob wasn't real impressed, but, jeez, his dad's alright, you know. Besides, we didn't mind, we'd been at it for hours."

"And?" Cassie prompted. "Then what?"

"Then I dropped Bryce and Ivan off at home." He stopped and shrugged. "I *thought* I went straight home myself. But then how did I end up dead?"

"Good question. We need to track your movements after you left the party. Someone must know where you went."

"But I wouldn't have gone anywhere. I was heading home. That's what, three, maybe four blocks away?" He started to pace. Cassie watched in amazement as his shape slid in and out of focus with his movements. Finally, she couldn't stand it anymore. "Stop it, will you? You're making me dizzy."

Pulling up beside her, so close the tiny scar at the base of his jaw was visible, he sat down on the other swing. It never moved under his weight. Her gaze switched from the swing to him and then back again. The rusted chain links shone right through him.

"Todd, you said you'd seen other dead people—"

"Some are dead." He shrugged, unconcerned.

Cassie stared. "I can see how you may not want to dwell on this stuff, but me, I'm just a little confused. You said some of those people are dead – but some aren't?"

He shifted sideways in the swing. Cassie shivered, a little creeped out that the chains didn't shift. "I don't know what the others are. I haven't been here long enough to know anything, remember?"

"I just wondered. Can any of them help you?"

"Help me, how?"

Cassie knew it would sound stupid, but well, she just had to ask. "Todd, is dead forever? Or can you come back?"

He laughed. "Come back? Like a mistake happened and I shouldn't be dead? Or do something righteous and be allowed to return?" He shook his head. "I don't think it works that way. I think dead is dead."

"Oh." Tears threatened. She choked them back. Cassie hated to think his young life was over. He deserved so much more. She wanted him alive again.

"That means a lot to me, you know?"

She glanced sideways in his direction, holding back a sniffle. "What does?"

"That you'd like me back. You're the only one who cares enough to want that."

Cassie wiped her eyes on her sleeve. "Your dad would, I'm sure."

"Hell, no. He doesn't care. He's probably happy I'm gone." Todd laughed, a bitter sound that made her wince. "You know what he's like."

She gave a little shrug. She didn't like his father much, but that was because Adam Spence didn't appreciate his son. Cassie ached for both of them. Typical males. They grunted in passing. And somehow that was good enough for them. Girls talked about everything. And if they ran out of things to talk about, they started all over again.

"Well, I miss you, but I'm glad you're here in this—" She wafted her hand toward his nonphysical form. "Condition."

Todd laughed, reached out a hand to cover hers. "Thanks, I think."

She glanced at their joined hands, his was cool to the touch. Staring up at him, knowing her pain shone clear in her eyes, she said, "I don't want to lose you – again – but if I have to, I want to make the most of this time. And I'll help you figure out what happened on the night you died, but I want you to do something for me."

He frowned. "Like what? I'm not exactly capable of doing much, you know."

But he was. "Learn the world you're in. How it works. Maybe speak to these other people. Ask them questions, like how long you get to stay here? And can you hang with me all day, every day?" Which couldn't be possible for everyone or Grams would be here, too.

He laughed. "I know which one I'd prefer." Todd stood, slipped his hands into his front jeans pockets with his thumbs sticking out, a mannerism that was so him. His lips quirked. "Thanks for caring, kiddo."

Just then his face started to shimmer, thinning, fading. Cassie cried out. "No, wait. Don't go. Please." She stood up, taking several steps toward him, one hand outstretched.

"Love ya, Cassie." His form wavered, thinned, then disappeared.

Cassie sat on her swing for another hour, waiting, hoping he'd come back. She still had so many unasked questions.

He didn't. Still, as she headed back home, she felt much better, her heart much lighter.

Todd might be dead, but he was still here. For her. For now.

CHAPTER THREE

Cassie phoned Rob, one of Todd's best friends and, by extension, one of hers, as she took the boulevard toward home.

"Hey, this is Cassie. Did you hear about Todd?" She stopped to wait for the traffic light to change before crossing. A chilly breeze swooped down, forcing her to tug the edges of her hoodie together.

"Yeah, I called you earlier, but you didn't answer. I posted to your Facebook wall and figured you'd answer when you got a chance."

Cassie grimaced as she stepped up on the sidewalk. "Sorry about that. I didn't want to talk to anyone. I haven't been online for the same reason. This has been a terrible time for me."

"It's messed up, man. Todd hardly drank, and when he did, he never drove. I don't get it." His voice choked up.

"So, you heard he'd been drinking and driving, too?"

Rob cleared his throat. "Yeah, that's what everyone's saying."

She didn't dare mention seeing Todd's ghost. She needed to watch that. Her parents would have her at the shrink's and on medication before dinnertime if it came up again. "What happened that night?"

"Nothing. We were playing like we always do, then my dad came home and the boys shipped out. No drinking. No drugs. No girls. It was normal."

That confirmed Todd's story. "Any idea what time that was?" Cassie zipped her hoodie closed, unable to stop shivering.

She'd been cold while she was speaking with Todd too. Did his arrival always come with a cold breeze? After a quick search around, hoping to see Todd, she crossed the road to continue her walk in the sun.

"Somewhere around ten-thirty or eleven, I think. Todd drove the others home. I've already spoken to them. They said they went straight home and have no idea where Todd went afterward."

"That's so odd."

A lone car drove slowly behind Cassie. She turned, but didn't recognize it. She picked up her pace. It pulled up to the curb beside her.

"Cassie?"

Cassie twisted at the voice. "Rob, I'll call you back. Ivan just pulled up." She clicked off her cell and walked over. She bent down to peer through the passenger window. The window lowered. She smiled at another of Todd's friends. "Hey. I guess you passed your driver's test, huh? Is this your mom's car?"

"Yeah. Did you hear about Todd?"

Cassie sighed. Already she wasn't looking forward to the next few days. "Yeah, I did. I was just on the phone with Rob about it. Todd dropped you off last night, didn't he?"

Ivan switched off the car engine. "Yeah. We dropped Bryce off first, then me. And before you ask, we didn't go anywhere and neither did we drink..." He grimaced. "This is pretty tough. Todd was a decent guy – most of the time."

He didn't need to elaborate. There was no getting around the fact that Todd was a bit of wild card, and that's what people would remember.

Cassie knew the real Todd. Not too many other people did or cared to. Unlikely friends, they'd both needed someone and had been overjoyed to find each other.

"I'm going to miss him." She straightened. Would Ivan know more than Rob? "He didn't say if he was going anywhere else after you guys called it a night, did he?" At Ivan's mystified look, she shrugged. "I just can't believe what everyone is saying. Besides, it's not like there was time after dropping you off either."

"I know. It's crazy. But I don't know what he did after I said good night." Ivan turned the car on again. "Do you want a ride home?"

She shook her head, not comfortable getting into the car with a new driver. Todd had been an excellent driver, had driven her everywhere, and look what happened to him. "I'm good. I need to walk and think things over."

"Right. See you at school."

He drove off slowly, steadily, as if aware that this metal-and-plastic-and-glass car that felt so safe could be smashed in an instant. And his body – skin and bones and heart – could as easily be crushed. That, like Todd, he could be dead in a heartbeat.

Too bad Todd's death wouldn't stop other people from drinking and driving...and dying.

***

Todd watched his old friend drive away. When had Ivan gotten his license? Crap, that's right, Ivan's test had been the morning after – Saturday morning – this morning. Todd had missed it. He'd been bugging Ivan about his upcoming test for weeks. At least Ivan had passed.

His brows came together in a frown. He'd wanted to be there to cheer him on.

Being dead sucked.

And he had yet to figure out how this appearance and disappearance thing worked. Like how could Cassie see him, but no one else? He'd gone to his mom's house, but neither she nor his brother Jessie appeared to notice him. His dad seemed to sense something, but not necessarily in a good way. Then again, the old man was a useless drunk. Since Todd's accident, he seemed to have gone over the edge.

Now, as a ghost, sometimes Todd could imagine himself at one location and find himself there instantly. At other times he had to walk there. His feet didn't touch the ground. He'd tried to travel a foot above the ground, which worked just fine, too. He could sit down and not sink into the objects, yet sometimes they went right through him. Picking up stuff didn't work either.

He shook his head. Whether he liked it or not, this was where he was for the moment. Knowing the laws here would help. Unfortunately, no one had offered him a book of rules and instructions for ghosts.

Cassie strolled ahead of him, texting on her cell phone. He wished he knew who she was contacting. It should be him. He missed her calls. She'd text him if class was boring, the coffee was good and even with comments friends made. No more.

He hated it. Hated the loneliness. Hated feeling lost. Hated being dead.

Across the street some homeless looking dude was staring at her. The guy wore a stupid lecherous grin on his face and when Cassie strolled away he turned to watch. That pissed Todd off. No losers should be allowed to look at someone as decent as Cassie. Todd snarled in his direction, "What the hell are you looking at?"

The guy widened his grin, gave him the finger and walked down the street.

Todd glared. Asshole. Spinning around again, he found Cassie had disappeared around the corner. He stopped. Wait, that guy had understood him. He'd seen and heard him. Todd spun around.

The homeless guy was gone.

Shit.

School on Monday sucked. Cassie had spent most of Sunday waiting, hoping that Todd would show up. No such luck. She avoided her friends. She didn't want to talk about him, she wanted to talk *to* him. She still didn't understand what had happened on Todd's last night either.

"Cassie?"

Cassie spun around and came up against the crush of people racing behind her. But that voice?

"Cassie?"

Todd's younger brother, Jessie, stepped in front her. Cassie's hopes deflated, but at the same time her heart lightened. Seemed like she'd had a crush on Jessie since forever. He lived with Todd's mom on the other side of town. She hadn't spent much time with him, but he'd always been nice to her. Besides, he was deadly cute.

Todd hated that Jessie was a warmer version of himself. Jessie was so much more than that. Jessie had broader shoulders, was slightly taller and very approachable. Add in Jessie's lopsided grin and those chocolate sun-kissed curls...she almost sighed. She caught the sound at the last minute, but still felt heat rise up her neck.

Blinking hard, she gave Jessie a friendly smile, loving the instant response on his face. Jessie had tried to be friendly, to connect as family to Todd, but divorce – with each parent taking one kid – didn't do much for brotherly love. "Jessie, how are you holding up?"

He glanced down at the cement floor. His curls, so like his brother's, fell forward the same way Todd's had. He swallowed.

Tears came to her eyes. She hastily looked away, blinking several times.

Jessie shifted to one side to get out of the way as they were once again engulfed by a crowd. "I'm okay. It's been tough, though. I wished I'd gotten to know him better. Wished we'd had more time to grow up and get out of all that family crap. Maybe we could've been closer."

When Grams died, Cassie had been obsessed with all the plans they'd made together that would never come to pass. She understood Jessie's pain. "How's your mom doing?"

He snorted. "She alternates between blaming Dad and then herself for Todd going bad."

Cassie stiffened. "Dying in a car accident is hardly a case of having gone bad."

"It is when he's been drinking and driving. Or didn't you know that part?"

"I've heard the rumors, but I don't believe everything I hear. I spent a lot of time with Todd, and he never drank around me, nor did I ever see him drive after he'd been drinking." Cassie's temper flashed and was followed almost immediately by a twinge of disappointment that Jessie had automatically believed the rumors. "All the friends he'd been with that night said there'd been no alcohol involved."

The bell rang and the two slowly made their way to the end of the hall.

Cassie, still slightly indignant on Todd's behalf, remained quiet.

"His friends could by lying, but I hope the police find evidence that proves you're right," Jessie said. "As for my mom, well, she's been through this before with my dad, so she believes that Todd followed his father's footsteps."

At the door to Cassie's chemistry class, she stopped to study his face. "Forget about what she thinks. You're what, sixteen?"

"Almost seventeen. Todd was only sixteen months older."

Loyalty for Todd demanded some kind of defense. "Maybe you didn't know your brother all that well, but didn't you know him enough to decide for yourself what he would've done?" She stepped around the corner, narrowly avoiding being run down by other students. "I do. And I choose to believe in Todd. He *didn't* do what they say he did."

"But the police already determined that he'd been driving under the influence," he protested.

"Then it's up to us to prove them wrong." With that Cassie turned and entered into the chaos of the science room, leaving a stunned Jessie behind.

***

Jessie watched through the doorway as Cassie took her seat. She'd always been so careless of her popularity, not really seeing it for the gift it was. Genuinely nice girls weren't always popular. And her association with his brother probably kept her from being one of the 'in' crowd, but she never seemed to notice – nor did anyone else. Todd had had only good things to say about her. Apparently they'd been best friends, whatever that meant to Todd.

She had to be hurting.

Hell, he was hurting.

And not a little bit because of her comment. Was he doing his brother a disservice by believing what he'd been told? Todd had learned to question life earlier than Jessie had. Living with Dad had been a crash course in survival.

Jessie's life had been easier, gentler. Still, being raised to respect authority, including law enforcement, didn't mean he couldn't question them or their conclusions. He wished he'd thought to do so when the deputy had stood on his front doorstep a couple of days ago. But he'd been too stunned to do anything but blink at the shocking news.

"Hell," he said aloud to the empty hallway, "I should've asked questions." He frowned. Maybe he still could. He certainly didn't remember the guy's name. How did one go chasing down an officer, anyway?

"Jessie? Aren't you supposed to be in class?"

Jessie came out of his musings to see Vice Principle Jenner standing in front of him, his brow furrowed in concern. With no hair above those creases, his face looked like a wrinkled orange. Jessie sighed. "Sorry. I'm a bit out of it today."

Mr. Jenner's face softened. "That's understandable. Sorry to hear about your brother. That's a tough one to deal with on any day. Do you need to go home?"

Jessie hated the sympathy. What was he supposed to do with it? Say 'thanks'? For what? That his brother was dead? Or should he say it didn't matter? Like hell. It did matter. "I'm fine. I need to get to class, before I end up in trouble with my teacher."

With a nod, Mr. Jenner stepped aside to let Jessie pass. "Let me know if you're having problems adjusting, okay?"

Jessie lifted his hand in acknowledgment. That wasn't going to happen. He had enough trouble now. There'd been more talk about grief counselors coming. That didn't make any sense to him.

It didn't change anything. His brother was still dead.

Cassie couldn't pay attention. The periodic table wasn't cutting it today. She sighed and shifted back slightly. Her phone vibrated. She checked it and glanced over at Suzie, who grinned at her. Cassie nodded 'yes' to the text suggesting coffee after class. She shouldn't have been so snippy with Jessie, but everything and everyone pissed her off at the moment. Talk about a short fuse. Being with her friends might get her out of this dark mood.

The teacher droned on and Cassie, sitting in the sun, barely kept her eyes open. Ten more minutes, that's all she had to put up with. She glanced out at the sunshine. The soccer field raced with colors as two teams paired up to trounce each other. Todd had loved soccer. Darn. That's all she could think about.

A noise distracted her. Her gaze drifted around the room, picking up the whisperers and the gigglers in the back. What were they laughing at? Her glance carried to the other side of the room. And she saw him..

Todd.

Turning back around, she brought a hand up to hide the heat climbing her cheeks. What was he doing here, in her chemistry class? He wouldn't have been caught dead inside this room when he was alive, yet now that he was dead he was trying out the subject? That so didn't make any sense. She carefully glanced at the students around Todd. No one said anything. Or acted any different. Didn't they see him?

She studied Mr. Barrels, the chemistry teacher. He stared in Todd's direction. And didn't notice him. Cautiously Cassie turned her head to see if he was still there.

He waved, a big grin on his face. She automatically waved back, her eyes widening in shock as she realized what she'd done. Todd's devilish grin widened and he laughed. Cassie pivoted and kept her head locked in that position, knowing her cheeks had to be bright red by now.

"What's the matter, Cassie?" whispered Tess from behind.

Cassie shrugged, not daring to speak or turn for a third time. Darn Todd anyways. He was going to get her in trouble. No sooner had the thought occurred then she chastised herself. Todd was dead. He wasn't *doing* anything. And how sad was that?

Finally the bell rang and drowned out Mr. Barrel's monotone voice droning on and on about chemical compounds. He was still speaking as the first kids bolted for the door. Cassie took her time. If Todd was still there, she needed to composed herself, or she'd walk right up and speak to him. To everyone else, she'd be talking to the door because that's where he'd been standing. She groaned. This couldn't be good. She so wasn't any good at keeping secrets.

Tess waited for her to gather up her books. "Are you alright? You were acting weird."

Cassie tried to smile. "I'm fine. Or I will be. I keep seeing Todd everywhere, or expecting to see him," she amended quickly.

Tess's face scrunched up with compassion. "Oh, that's so sad. You two were so close."

"Yeah. I probably shouldn't have come in today. I haven't been able to keep my mind on anything. I'm just going to have to read these notes over again at home."

"Stay home tomorrow. You're a good student. One day won't make a difference."

Cassie couldn't find a smile for that. One day *had* made all the difference – and not for the better.

CHAPTER FOUR

Jessie hurried home. He was due at work in an hour, but he'd hoped to have time to talk to his mom first. He found her collapsed in her favorite chair in the sunroom, her face red and puffy.

He sighed. "Hi Mom."

She sniffled back tears and gave him a watery smile. "Hi, honey. How did school go?"

He dropped his backpack on the floor and pulled up the footstool in the middle of the room. Rolling closer, he reached out and picked up her hand. "School was okay. Everyone's talking about Todd. To be expected, I guess."

She tried to straighten up. After a moment of unsuccessful effort she collapsed back down. "I'm sorry. It's all my fault. I shouldn't have broken up the family like I did."

"Oh, Mom, no one could have predicted this."

A frown wrinkled through her tears. "I should have. Look at his father. I should never have allowed Adam to take him, but he loved Todd so much. They were so close, then. Todd helped stabilize Adam." She sniffled. "You've ended up so much better than Todd."

"Did we really know him?" Jessie couldn't help but remember Cassie. She'd seemed so adamant, so sure of Todd. Yet he, Todd's own brother, wasn't. "Are you so sure he was the kind of person who'd drink and drive?"

Confusion blinked in her eyes. "What else is there to think?" She straightened successfully this time. Leaning forward, she patted his hand. "The police told us what happened."

"I know they did. I…it's just I'd like to make sure. Do you remember who came to the door and spoke to us?" Jessie searched his mother's face.

She frowned. "Honey, I don't think there's been a mistake."

He bent his head. "I know. I just want to talk to him. Ask a few questions. Make sure. I don't want to think back on this and wish I'd done more."

Unshed tears glowed in her eyes. "Then call him. His card is on the table." Pride slowly crept into her gaze. "You're such a good boy for having thought of it."

Jessie smiled. "You would have eventually. That's why I want to do this now, so there're no doubts later on." He stood up and walked to the table, snagging the card on his way.

***

"Cassie, it's dinner time."

Cassie groaned and closed her eyes again. She didn't care about food. She didn't care about school. She didn't care about anything. She just wanted everything and everyone to go away.

Her mom's voice came again, gratingly loud. "Cassie, come on."

Sitting upright, Cassie threw off her blanket and walked to her mirror. She winced at her reflection. Picking up a brush, she ran it through her hair. As she started to close the door to her room, she cast yet another glance at the same corner where she'd seen Todd. It was empty. Again. She'd looked dozens of times, called for him twice as many times, and still there was no sign of him.

Her stomach clenched. Maybe he couldn't visit anymore.

She headed down to dinner. Sensing her parents studying her as she ate, she kept her head down and worked through her plate. Everything tasted like cardboard. But there'd be fewer questions this way. When she was done, she stood up and went to wash the dishes. Her father started to say something, then stopped.

Her mother's doing probably. Cassie didn't care. Finishing the dishes, she headed upstairs, maintaining her silence. Once in her room, she flung herself down on her bed and closed her eyes.

The phone rang downstairs. "Cassie, it's for you."

She rolled her eyes. Great. Picking up the phone in the hallway, she yelled, "Got it, Mom." She took the phone back into her room. "Hello."

"Cassie? This is Jessie."

Cassie frowned as she plunked back down on her bed. "Hi."

"Look, I thought about what you said."

She fell back against the pillows and groaned. "And what was that?" She barely kept the sarcasm in control.

He took a deep breath. "As much as I hate to say it - you were right. I didn't question anything I was told. And..." He paused. "I realize I should have."

Cassie raised her eyebrows and rolled her eyes. Yes, he should have. "I'm glad." He laughed, a mocking sound that made her wince. "I'm sorry. I didn't mean to be snarky. I'm not having a great day."

"No, it's alright. I deserved it. I'm sorry for not being there for him. But I wanted to tell you that I called the sheriff's office."

"You did?" Cassie bolted upright. "What did they say?"

He cleared his throat. "The deputy said that Todd was the only person around the vehicle."

"Around? You mean he wasn't found in it?"

"No. He was found clear of the vehicle, either from being thrown out or he crawled off a ways."

"Oh," Cassie said in a small voice, as horrible images rushed through her mind. Todd bouncing from the crashed vehicle or worse images of Todd crashing but alive and crawling out of the vehicle, only to die alone from his injuries.

"They found broken bottles and alcohol all over the interior of the vehicle. He was also covered in the stuff."

Cassie let out a small cry.

Jessie rushed to add, "The deputy also said he wouldn't have suffered long. His injuries were severe enough he wouldn't have known what was going on."

"That helps a little." Cassie took a deep breath, willing the tears back. She blinked furiously. "I'd hate to think of him hurt and alone, waiting for someone to come." She took a second breath, this one coming easier. "They're sure he was all alone?"

"That's what they said. They have laid the blame on Todd's head and his alone."

Cassie closed her eyes. Hot tears ran down her cheeks, unchecked. "I'd hoped for something different."

"I know. Me, too." Jessie voice deepened. "I asked him several times if someone could have walked away from the accident."

Cassie's eyes opened wide. "Oh. What did he say?"

"He said it was unlikely."

"Unlikely, but not impossible?" Hope bubbled up inside. Finally. Something positive. Progress. She grinned.

Jessie's voice dampened her optimism. "That wasn't a yes."

"I don't care. I'm sure there had to be someone else driving. Now to prove it."

"Whoa! Cassie, what are you talking about?"

Should she tell him? About seeing Todd as a ghost?

Hell no!

She shifted into a cross-legged position, transferring the phone to her right hand. Dropping her free hand to the comforter, she traced the geometric pattern on her bedspread while working out the problem. He might believe her, but not likely. "He was my friend. I know he didn't do this and I want to clear his name."

"Cassie?"

Jessie had to wonder what chaos he'd started. "You don't have to believe me," she rushed in to say. "I know you didn't know him the way I did, but—"

"But I wish I did." Jessie sighed heavily. "It's not lost on me that you knew him so much better and believed in him, while his own family blindly accepted his guilt."

"Then help me. Help me prove his innocence."

"Why? It's not going to change anything. He's still dead."

"Is he? Do you think he isn't here in spirit? Wouldn't he want us to do this for him?" Cassie stood up and walked over to the window and pulled back the blinds. Night had settled in. She leaned on the edge of the frame and stared out in the blackness. "If it had been me, I'd want someone to clear my name."

***

Todd sat on Cassie's window ledge, alternately staring out into the night and watching Cassie as she slept. He could have spoken with her when he'd popped in earlier, but he'd arrived during her phone call – to his brother, no less. It had saddened him. And it had bugged the hell out of him. He'd never taken the time to really connect with Jessie when he was alive. Now he found it was one more in the long list of things he regretted, now that it was too late to do anything about them.

It figures.

Cassie's dark blond hair fanned across the pillow. Her face was puffy and swollen from the tears he'd watched fall earlier. A private scene she'd not have appreciated him seeing. His heart hurt. For her. For his brother. And most of all for himself.

He hadn't meant to die. In fact, he hadn't realized he had until he was in the morgue, listening to the strange conversation going on around him. A conversation he'd been horrified to learn was about him.

He had *not* been drinking and driving. And he didn't give a shit what they said – they were wrong.

Many people had seen him as a wild case doomed to an early end. But that wasn't true. That had been his front, his bravado to hide the million insecurities inside.

He loved Cassie – maybe even more now. The loving family he'd never had... There was just something about not being the one chosen to stay with his mother that had never quite healed. He'd understood – sorta. After all, Jessie was the younger kid. He'd needed Mom more. Todd was already more independent and through the divorce, more bitter. Older. He'd started to try things, experimenting like so many others of his age. But never drinking and driving – at least, not together.

He wished he could remember. Why would he have done something like that? If he'd done it? It was a stupid stunt. Of all the things he might have called himself, stupid wasn't one of them.

Thankfully he had Cassie in his corner. Or maybe he was in Cassie's corner.

She believed in him. He'd been friendly with many kids – of all kinds, just never the popular 'in' group. That was his insecurity speaking, his need to be admired. His lack of confidence required people's friendship, affirming he was worthy. Surely that many people couldn't be wrong – could they? Especially not Cassie.

For that he was grateful. He walked over to the bed where she slept and leaned down to run his fingers through her hair. He'd never put on airs around Cassie. He hadn't needed to. She alone, knew the real him, including all his dark places. She shifted, murmuring in her sleep, sensing him even then.

No one else could see him. No one else cared to.

No one but her.

***

Adam Spence reached for another beer from the pack beside him. The six he'd brought home hadn't even made it to the fridge. No point now, he was drinking the last one. "I don't know what to do for the funeral," he said into the phone.

Sandra, his nag of an ex-wife, wouldn't leave him alone. All he wanted to do was forget…and she wouldn't let him.

"He lived with you. Are you going to make the arrangements or not?" Her voice sounded rough. Probably too many hours crying. Blaming him. That was his life these days.

Groaning aloud, he popped the top and took a healthy swig. "I don't know what to do. You handle it. He was your son, too." Silence. He sighed. "Look, you make the arrangements and I'll pay the bills and show up." When she didn't answer, he figured that was a yes. Damn straight. "Good. Then let me get back to my drinking. I have some serious forgetting to do tonight."

"Is that all you care about? What about your other son? Did you ever think that he might need you right now?"

"Jessie? Hell, he can't stand me and you know it. He probably wishes I'd died instead of Todd."

Sandra started to cry softly. "If he does it's because you've never spent any quality time with him. The boy needs a strong father figure."

"Not this father." Adam slammed the phone down and opened his throat, pouring the beer straight back. That was the problem with beer. It took too many to get a buzz on. He staggered to his feet, heading for the pantry and the bottle of whiskey he was sure he'd stashed there.

Pulling it out, he gloated. That was more like it. He opened the cap and drank straight from the bottle. "Maybe now I won't see my boy every damn time I turn around."

He turned and fell onto the couch to stare out into the lonely black of night. The pain just wouldn't quit. No matter how much he drank. Tilting the bottle again, he kept one eye on the vision of his son leaning against the porch door, his thumbs hooked into his jeans as always, with that mocking look on his face.

"Go away. Stop haunting me." The bottle upended once more, emptying the last of the molten gold liquid. Angrily, he threw it at the vision.

Todd jumped out of the way with a laugh as the bottle bounced off the wall behind him. A laugh Adam swore he could hear.

CHAPTER FIVE

Tuesday morning it rained.

Gray sheets filled the skies. Cassie stared out her bedroom window. She'd planned to wear a beautiful new t-shirt. Rain was not part of the program. Just then, Penny texted her. Cassie smirked. Penny was impressed by the weather, too. Not.

Time had slipped away from Cassie. She needed to get moving or she'd be late for class. She'd spent too long on Facebook already this morning. Even dead, Todd was still the topic of choice amongst her friends.

Penny waited for her at the front doors of the school. Cassie grinned at her curvy friend. The guys flocked around Penny every chance they could, but turned tail and ran when they understood her seriously scary brainpower. And Penny was as nice as she was smart.

Cassie hadn't meant to ignore her all weekend; she just hadn't been able to talk to anyone – which wasn't fair. Penny, although not a big Todd fan, was a Cassie fan and would understand how much she hurt.

Her friend watched her, concern shining from her hazel eyes.

"Hey." Cassie linked an arm around her friend's shoulders. "Sorry. I've had a tough couple of days."

"Yeah, I noticed." Penny squeezed Cassie's arm. "Glad to see you looking more like yourself." The two walked in, arms linked, heads almost touching.

"I'm getting there, but slowly," admitted Cassie. "It's hard listening to what everyone else is saying about him. I know they didn't know him like I did, but I didn't expect people to go totally off on him, either. My dad's been snarky mean about Todd since the accident. It hurts"

"Dads are like that and yours hated Todd. He's probably happy Todd's dead."

Cassie stumbled. It sounded so wrong to hear people say things like that. She knew Todd was gone physically, but her heart and mind couldn't quite accept it. Not while she could still see and talk with him. But neither did she understand his current state. She lived in fear he'd disappear and never return. She hadn't seen him since class yesterday. And that worried her.

"Wow, aren't you two cute?" Kendra, with a big blond brute-of-a-guy at her side, walked up to the two girls. Cassie stiffened.

"Easy. Don't let her get to you," cautioned Penny, keeping Cassie's arm tight against her. "She's just trying to piss you off."

"I know," murmured Cassie, eyeing Kendra. "She's succeeding. If she says one thing about Todd, I'm going—"

"So your little Toddy bear killed himself, did he?" She snickered, sending a knowing look at the brawny brain-dead male at her side. "Drinking and driving. What an ass."

"Cassie—" Penny warned, but it didn't stop Cassie.

"Todd wasn't drinking and driving, and if you knew him as well as you'd like everyone else to think you did…" Cassie's smirk grew at the outrage on Kendra's face. "Then you'd remember how strict he was on that issue."

"I knew Todd better than you ever did, you. How dare you imply anything else? Todd loved me. You were nothing to him." Kendra's face turned a mottled red.

Penny tugged hard on Cassie arm, dragging her down the hallway. "Don't say anything. Do you want to get in trouble? She's a bitch. Always has been and always will be. I don't know what Todd saw in her."

Cassie snorted. "Todd didn't see anything *in* her. He couldn't get past the assets sticking out in *front* of her."

Penny snickered. "So true. But he was male."

"You and I both know why she's so popular, but the guys don't get it. Todd couldn't tell me what he liked about her. The conversation always came back to what he could get *from* her."

"I can't believe you two talked about things like that."

"We talked about everything. That's why it hurts so bad. You have your mom. I just don't have that type of relationship with mine. I'm always afraid she'll involve my dad somehow. And he's always so furious when boys are mentioned. You know how he was with Todd." She scrunched up her face and mimicked, "He's too old for you. He's too worldly for you. He's too…He's too…" She groaned. "Ohh, he never shuts up."

Penny giggled. "And what you hate is he's often right. Todd was too old for you. He was all those other things as well, but your dad didn't understand. Todd was a special friend. He wasn't your boyfriend."

It was so nice to be understood. Penny and Cassie had fights over the ten years that they'd known each other, but that had settled down as they'd grown older and decided to be friends in spite of their differences, in the same way she'd built her relationship with Todd.

Todd had talked about his girlfriends, and Cassie had asked him tons of questions about boys he knew. The insider knowledge had been great for her and her friends.

Who did she have now?

Taking her seat in English class, Cassie looked around and realized that she had loads of friends, but few really good ones. Penny was the closest of three. Todd had been the lone male in her circle.

She frowned as a paper airplane landed on her desk. Scribbles covered one wing.

Todd was a loser and he got what he deserved.

Her back stiffened. How dare people talk about him like that? Todd hadn't been a loser. People may have had that impression of him but they didn't *know* him.

The English teacher walked in, a note in his hand. "I'm to tell you that the funeral for Todd Spence is this Friday afternoon at four, for those of you who wish to go and pay your respects. I'll post this information on the board."

Tears sprang to Cassie's eyes as words of protest sprang to her mouth. She choked them back. She bowed her head, her fists clenched in her lap. Todd was dead. His body – that part of him – would need to be buried. Staring down at her hands, she refused to look around. She felt the stares, heard the half whispers. How difficult to realize she might be the only one to show up on Friday. Well, his mom and brother would be there. So would Todd. If he could, that is.

Thoughts of him watching the ceremony brought a tiny smile to her face. He'd probably get a kick out of it. So far, though, he hadn't sounded particularly enthralled with the changes in his life. Not that she blamed him.

Maybe she'd search out Jessie at lunch time. See if he had any news.

With a plan in place, Cassie tuned back into class.

***

Todd stuck close to Cassie throughout the morning, interested in this side of her. She seemed one person with him and then another without him. Being dead gave him a unique look into her life. Normal for everyone, he supposed. Still, he'd been amazed at the spat between Kendra and Cassie. Kendra was a bitch, always had been, and obviously had no plans to change anytime soon.

But she'd 'put out' and that had been valuable. He grinned. Guys had needs, after all.

He'd always been protective of Cassie, but now he had a big-picture view. A view that highlighted different priorities, put things in an order of relevance he hadn't been able to see while he was alive.

He knew Cassie needed help to find the truth about his accident. But who? The only friends he'd trust around her were Bryce, Ivan and maybe Rob. But they wouldn't help. They were law abiding and respectful and would believe exactly what the police told them. They'd listen to Cassie and agree to her face, to make her happy, then say later that she was overreacting, and overemotional because of her grief.

His other so-called friends would laugh her off for the opposite reason. They didn't like cops, never believed what they said and avoided all cops.

Maybe his brother? He wasn't so sure he wanted those two together. Just the thought made his insides tumble around. Or they would, if he had insides.

He placed a hand on his belly and pushed inward. His hand want right though the vision of shirt material and skin. There was nothing there. Holding up his hand he could see people through his palm.

He wasn't solid.

Staring around the crowded classroom, he realized he couldn't smell that stuffy stale odor he had always picked up in this classroom. And if he couldn't smell, why could he hear and speak? Weird. Wonderful, yeah, sometimes – but the rest, well, he didn't quite know.

A funeral, huh? Funny, he'd never put any thought into his own death.

Odd to think that the first funeral he'd attend would be his own.

***

Lunchtime, as always, was nuts. Kids stayed in class to work on homework, others ran to the closest store for goodies, and all of them seemed to pass in front of, or around Cassie on the way to the commons room. She'd forgotten to pack a lunch. Well, not really. She hadn't bothered was more like it. She'd lost her appetite. She had to force food down when her parents were around or they'd get on her case, but when they weren't there...

"Can I treat you to an iced coffee?" Penny appeared at her elbow.

Cassie smiled. "That's a great idea. Thanks. Are you having one?"

"Duh, girlfriend. You think you're going to get away with drinking one of those in front of me? Of course, I am. Find us a place to sit and I'll be right back." Penny disappeared in the sea of jeans and purple hair. Cassie surveyed the large room and rolled her eyes. She should have gone to buy the drinks and left Penny to find a seat. This place was chaos.

Working her way down one wall, Cassie headed to the far corner of the large open room. Just as she was about to snag a corner foam cushion, a larger male plunked down in front of her.

Outrage didn't quite cover her reaction. Cassie narrowed her gaze and pinned Jessie in place. "A gentleman would let the lady have the seat, particularly as she was here first."

Several of Jessie's friends laughed and crowded around her.

"There're no gentlemen here, sweetheart."

"Uh, did you say a lady? Where?"

Their taunts wouldn't stop. She tossed them a withering look before looking for another space.

"Here, you can have it."

The guys' laughter stopped as if it had been sliced off. They stared down at Jessie. Jessie stood up and motioned at Cassie to take the chair. "You're right. You were here first. Take it, please."

Curious, Cassie stared at him.

He shifted, uncomfortable, either with her or with his chivalrous actions. Maybe those surprised him as much as they had everyone else.

"Thank you." She stepped forward and sat down.

The other guys backed off, following Jessie toward the back doors. "Why the hell did you do that?"

"Jesus, man, just because she was your brother's stupid girlfriend doesn't mean you have to go and give her our spot."

Todd's stupid girlfriend. Cassie could only wonder what else people thought of her relationship with Todd. A Principal's List student, she hardly qualified for 'stupid' status. Obviously people applied the term because she had been friends with Todd. Cassie slid lower in the seat and closed her eyes, letting other conversations drift around her. She'd much rather be home alone in her room.

"Cassie?"

She opened her eyes.

Todd. Looking as careless and gorgeous as always.

She bolted upright, glanced around and quickly sat back down. "What are you doing here?" Keeping an eye on anyone close enough to hear, Cassie winced at the idea of being overheard.

"Don't you want to see me?" He grinned.

She noted he wore the same clothes. Were they the ones he'd worn in the accident? If so, why weren't they covered in blood? Or alcohol, for that matter. Keeping her voice soft, she asked him.

"I don't know. These are all I've seen. I can't take them off." He tried to lift up the strap of his muscle shirt and it lifted but was as transparent as his own body. He hooked his fingers into his pockets and his fingers disappeared as if they were actually going into something. Weird.

"Your brother called a deputy, asking for more details."

"Oh." Todd sat on the arm of the couch, oblivious to everyone else.

Cassie couldn't talk out loud to the empty air in front of her face. People were worried about her now. Wait until she got caught talking to a piece of furniture.

"What did he find out?"

Keeping her voice low and trying not to move her lips too much – which wasn't easy – she relayed what she'd learned.

"I was outside the vehicle? So I must have been thrown free." He frowned. "That can't be right. I always wear a seatbelt. And what about the air bags, were they deployed?"

Cassie shook her head. "I don't know. He didn't mention them."

Todd stared off into the distance. "We need to find out. If the airbags did work, I had help getting out of the vehicle. I think they deflate quickly, but they're big and awkward. They would have been hard to get around. If they didn't, then maybe something mechanical was wrong with the car and that caused the accident."

Cassie pursed her lips. Odd, she hadn't considered a mechanical problem. Why not? If there'd been booze containers in the car, still in the case or bag, they would have obviously broken in the accident, spraying their contents throughout. Had the police considered that?

"I may have to call them myself."

"Call who?" Penny stood in front of her, two iced coffees in her hand, slightly out of breath.

Cassie glanced at Todd then shook her head. Todd was gone. Again.

"Here, take one will you? These things are freezing."

Cassie snagged the one on the left and took a long sip, hoping her friend wouldn't notice her discomfort. Penny took Todd's spot. Cassie watched her out of the corner of her eye, wondering if she'd feel anything different. Nope.

"The line was huge." Penny shook her shoulder-length, brown hair – the ends flipped up as they landed. "At least I can sit down now."

"Mmmm." Cassie busied herself drinking her iced treat.

"So, who are you going to call?"

Glancing up at her friend, Cassie shrugged. "I might call the police and ask for the facts about Todd's death."

"Oh, no. Don't do that. You're never going to get over this if you have all those nasty details rolling around in your head." Penny pretended to shiver horribly. "Yuck."

"I know, but I need answers and I won't get them unless I ask."

"Ask his father, then. He'd know the important ones."

Cassie shuddered. She'd rather not know than approach Todd's father. She'd seen a lot of him over the years, and when the man was drunk, ugh. He was bad news. Then again, Jessie could ask him. They might be on talking terms. "Are you going to the funeral on Friday?"

Penny glanced sideways at her. "I don't want to. I hate funerals. Besides, I start work at four. I'd have to get someone to cover my shift, and you know how hard that is."

Penny was a part-time checker at Thrifty's, and no one ever wanted to work Friday nights. Just the same, Cassie hoped Penny found someone to cover for her.

She wanted her by her side at the funeral. And she wanted answers to her questions.

Why was someone holding back information? Cassie was sure someone knew what happened to Todd on his last night, and she was going to find that person.

She needed to know the truth. And so did Todd.

***

Cassie walked into the sheriff's office on her way home from school. Going through the front door wasn't too bad, but once inside she felt intimidated. Everyone had such stern, imposing looks on their faces. Unapproachable. She almost backed out.

"Hi there. How can we help you?"

Cassie followed the sound of a friendly voice to a large counter where a woman smiled at her. A friendly face. Cassie headed for her, relief in her voice as she said, "I want to find out some information about an accident that happened last weekend."

The woman looked at her monitor and typed in something. "What kind of information are you looking for? And which accident?"

Cassie took a deep breath and gave out the details. "I'm…" she stumbled and corrected herself, "… I was his best friend and well, I can't sleep for the questions rolling around in my head."

"How old are you, Cassie?"

"Sixteen," she muttered, hoping age wouldn't make a difference.

"And do your parents know that you're here?"

A heavy sigh slid out. "No. And I suppose you can't talk to me unless they are here, too, huh?"

"That's not mandatory. Let me find someone for you." The woman stood and left the room.

Cassie wiped her sweaty hands on her jeans. That wasn't so bad.

"Cassie, come on through here. Deputy Magnusson has a few moments to spare."

The large wooden desk-high gate opened, giving Cassie entrance to the other side of the counter. The woman led her down a small hallway and into a smaller office. A portly man her father's age stood and smiled at her. "Come in, come in. We don't get too many people your age in here voluntarily, you know."

Cassie grimaced. "Not sure I'll ever come again either, sir."

He laughed. "Sit down and relax. What can I do for you?"

"Thank you." She sat down on the edge of the spare chair. "My friend, Todd, died in a car accident Friday night." Tears threatened. Cassie stopped, sniffled once and stared out the window for a long moment before she managed to get her emotions back under control. Facing the deputy again, she saw empathy and understanding on his face. "I know that everyone says he'd been drinking and driving and deserved what he got." This time tears did form in her eyes. She choked them back. "But, he didn't. He'd never drink and drive."

Deputy Magnusson sat back, crossed his hands on his belly and gave her a solid look. "First off, no young man deserves to die. So what they're thinking along that line is just plain wrong. Second, the investigation hasn't officially been closed and rumors will always float around."

"I need to make sure you checked out a few things."

The deputy raised one eyebrow and settled back into his chair. "Fire away and we'll see if I can help."

"Did his airbag go off?" she blurted out. Sitting back, she wondered at the frown on his face.

"You know, that's a darn good question. There was one on the car, I know that. And it was burned in the fire." He reached into the drawer at his side and pulled out a thin file. "I'm not sure if I have anything written down about whether it went off first though. Why are you asking?"

"I'm wondering if he was actually thrown out of the vehicle, and if he was, how? He kept his car tuned up particular. He loved that machine and there were airbags in it. So if the airbags went off, how could he have been thrown out of the vehicle?" she asked reasonably. "Also, did anyone find Todd's cell phone?"

The Deputy frowned as he flicked through his open file. "We didn't find one. Although, chances are it was destroyed in the fire."

Wincing, Cassie stared at the floor for a moment, catching her breath. "Right. Fire," she said weakly. "Was Todd burned as well?"

"No." He rushed to assure her. "He was far enough off to the side that he wasn't caught in the fire."

Her breath gusted out in relief, not wanting to have that picture locked into her head. "So is it possible for him to have been thrown out before the airbag opened up or to have crawled out after it inflated?"

The deputy studied her face. "What's the real problem here?"

Cassie flushed. "The problem is Todd didn't drink. Maybe a little but not very much and never ever would he drive afterward." She sighed. "Have you met his father?"

When the deputy nodded, she grimaced. "Maybe you don't know if you've never seen him at his worst, but Todd's dad is a horrible drunk with a matching drunk driving record. He hit a woman years ago when driving home. Todd never could accept the fact that his dad had gotten off so lightly." Raising her voice slightly, she repeated, "Todd would *never* drink and drive. Never. There had to have been someone else in that vehicle with him. Maybe they survived the crash and ran off, afraid of what they'd done. I don't know exactly what happened, but I need to." She leaned forward. "Please, check it out further."

With a heavy sigh, the deputy shuffled the papers in front of him, aimlessly. "I'll tell you what. We won't close the case until we have all the facts. Good enough?" At her bright smile, he held up a warning hand. "Don't get too excited. The men were pretty sure they knew how this accident had played out."

Cassie's grin didn't dim one bit. "No, I understand. Thank you." She jumped to her feet and headed for the door. At the doorway, she turned back. "I don't suppose it's possible to search for the cell phone is it? Just in case he picked up a friend who needed a ride or called for help?" She leaned over and handed him a folded sheet of paper with the type of phone, color and the number. "Here is the description of his phone. I've tried calling and texting, but it never goes through. Oh, and he scratched his initials on the back, on the sliding keyboard piece."

The deputy grinned. "Are you angling for a future in law enforcement, young lady?"

"No, sir. Just doing for a friend who can't do for himself."

Serious appreciation glinted in his eyes. "Lucky friend."

CHAPTER SIX

Cassie, can we see you for a few minutes, please," her mom called up to her.

Cassie groaned and dropped her head to her keyboard. When would they leave her alone? "Just a minute." She saved her homework, closed the lid on her laptop and headed downstairs. Checking her watch, she realized how late it had gotten.

Her parents sat on opposite sides of the kitchen table again. Her stomach sank. Now what? She studied their serious expressions. Would her life never get easier? "What's wrong?"

Her father spoke up. "On my way home from work, I saw you coming out of the sheriff's office."

Cassie stared up at the ceiling. Not good. She dropped her gaze to lock on his face and said, "And?"

"I'd like to know what you were doing there."

"Like to know or demanding to know?" She pulled out a chair and sat down. This might take awhile.

Abby jumped in. "Cassie, this isn't an interrogation. Honey, we're concerned about you. You've had a difficult time lately. And going to the sheriff's office is unusual for you."

"How do you know, Mom?" Cassie would have liked to ignore their glares, but found it beyond difficult. She always had. There was just something about that parental stare. "I wasn't trying to hide my visit there. I just didn't feel the need to tell you about it."

"Why did you go?" Abby got up and walked over to sit down beside her husband, aligning herself against Cassie, as always.

"I wanted answers about Todd's accident."

"Damn it!" Her father glared at her. "Why would you want to go and do that?"

Cassie's heart pounded. She rarely bucked her father. This time she had no choice. It was that important. Trying to keep her voice calm and steady, she said carefully, "Because I needed to."

Her dad sat back open-mouthed. Abby reached over and held his hand.

"Cassie, what information did you want?"

"Confirmation that no one else could have been driving that vehicle." The words just burst out. "I knew Todd. I knew him better than probably anyone else, and there's one thing that I know for sure – he wouldn't have gone driving *if* he'd been drinking."

Abby dropped her head. "Oh, honey. You're trying to prove he wasn't responsible. What difference will that make? He's still going to be gone. You have to accept that."

"All the difference in the world to me. Don't you understand? I go to school and all I hear throughout the day is how Todd brought this on himself. How Todd met the end he deserved. It doesn't stop." Her tone rose. "Todd. Did. Not. Do. This."

Slumped back into his chair, her dad stared at her wordlessly. Abby held her fist against her mouth.

"What will it take for you to leave this alone, Cassie?"

At the pain and caring in her mom's voice, Cassie's lower lip trembled.

"The truth."

***

Jessie kicked the rock all the way home, putting force behind the blows, enjoying the satisfaction of being able to hit something...hard. Tension lived with him these days. Nothing was the same anymore. He'd always been sure of what he wanted to do, knew where he wanted to go. That had changed. Everything felt messed up. His brother, he could have used more time with; and his father, well he could use a whole lot less of him. And his mom had grabbed the wrong idea there. She seemed to think he was missing a father's touch. That getting him and his dad together would save them both.

How wrong could she be? Todd was proof of that.

She was probably fearful that she might lose one of them or the other like she had Todd and she wanted them to have a relationship before it was too late. Like it now was with Todd.

But just because he'd lost his brother didn't mean he wanted to create a relationship with his messed up father.

His phone rang. Jessie checked the incoming text. Stephen and a couple of other friends wanted him to join them at the mall. He didn't feel like it. School was over for the day, and he felt lost. He wanted to know more about his brother. That meant talking to Cassie.

The tension inside eased. He'd always liked her, really liked her, but she'd been Todd's friend, and that had meant she'd been off limits. Todd's death was too recent to feel any differently about that. Yet, she'd always had a smile for him. Even more when Todd had acted like an ass. She'd always stepped in to smooth out any conflicts, the first to make everyone feel welcome.

It would be nice to talk to her.

His phone beeped again. He checked and didn't recognize the number. "Hello."

"Is this Jessie?"

"Yes, who is this?"

"Cassie. I grabbed your number off the phone when you called me."

Sweet. "Smart," he said.

"I stopped at the sheriff's office today and spoke to a deputy."

"Really? What did he say?"

Jessie listened in amazement as she explained what had gone down at the station. "Wow, I'm really surprised."

"I know. So am I, actually. It's encouraging."

"But he did say to not get excited about this," he warned. Jessie had to agree with that commonsense statement. To expect much out of this would be a mistake. He'd love to know that his brother hadn't done anything so stupid, but the odds were against confirming that.

"I know. I'm just happy they're at least going to check it out. They need to find his cell phone."

Jessie sat down on a bus stop bench. Cell phone? That's right. Todd was always on that thing. If the cops said he'd had an accident while texting, Jessie would have been convinced hands down.

Drunk driving – not so much.

"Jessie, are you there?"

"Yes, sorry." He sighed. "I just realized how much I'd blindly accepted. It never occurred to me that the police might not have retrieved the cell phone or checked out any calls."

"They haven't found it." Cassie's voice stopped and a weird sound carried through. "The deputy assumed the cell phone burned in the fire. He did say he'd consider the problem. See where Todd's phone might have ended up."

"What are you doing right now?" Jessie watched the traffic go by, not paying attention to anything but Cassie. He wanted to spend more time with her.

"I'm sipping coffee."

"Coffee?" Jessie gagged. The one time he'd tried the stuff he'd choked on it.

"Yeah, don't you drink it?" She giggled.

Jessie stared down at the phone in his hand, charmed. "Not really. Haven't had any that was drinkable."

She laughed aloud. "It took me a couple of tries before I liked it."

"Really?" Jessie didn't believe her, but he liked that she'd say so to make him more comfortable.

"Yeah. Come and try the coffee at the Shake Shop."

Jessie snorted. Several cars drove past, followed by a bus, which stopped beside him. "Doesn't sound like good advertisement for coffee." The bus stopped and let someone off. Jessie shook his head at the driver and waved him on. Cassie was still talking.

"I know. Weird, isn't it? But they make a good brew."

"Maybe I'll try it again one day."

"Why not today? That's where I am now. If there's one thing Todd's death showed me it's that we take every day for granted - instead of making the most of our time. Come and join me. I'm sitting by the window." With that she clicked off.

Jessie stared down at the phone; his pulse jumped for joy. Hell yeah, he'd try another cup of that poison if it meant hanging out with her. He stood up and headed off. In less than ten minutes, he'd be with Cassie. Of their own choice, his feet picked up the pace and raced down the street.

***

Deputy Magnusson read through the file on his desk. That pretty young lady had seemed so adamant. He had daughters of his own, and when they believed something, they were fanatical about it. Cassie Merchant had been passionate. She also looked to be a might stressed. Right or wrong, she'd presented some good arguments. He'd already checked out the boy's father. Sure enough he had a long history of charges, including domestic violence, traffic violations, along with several DUIs, ending in his running down a sixty-year old woman.

Cassie's facts were there, and her logic was sound. People growing up in that type of household often went to one extreme or the other. They'd either turn into alcoholics or never touch the stuff. According to Cassie, Todd fell into the latter group.

What Cassie was forgetting was the mentality of an eighteen-year-old, teenage male. Something no one could predict.

The cell phone was worth a second look. The airbag was something he wanted more information on, too. Had it inflated and deflated like it was supposed to? What about other mechanical problems? All in all, that young lady had brought up some valid points.

Where was the vehicle now? It should have been towed to the lot, but he didn't have that paperwork in front of him.

Why not?

***

Cassie sat in the corner of the Shake Shop and wondered what she'd just done – and why. Jessie had been on her mind all day. Even now her insides quivered at the idea he'd be here in a few minutes.

"Why the hell did you invite my brother here?"

Cassie started, letting out a small shriek. Todd sat across from her in the booth. She spun around to see if the older couple sitting behind them were listening in. "You have to stop doing that!" she hissed.

Todd glared. "What am I supposed to do, sing a song, tap you on the shoulder or something? Cripes, I'm darned happy to be able to even talk with you and you're nagging at me for the way I do it." He slouched in that way of his, and brooded.

Cassie grinned. Todd had brooding down pat. He'd have made it big in Hollywood.

He glanced at her, caught her grin and frowned. "What are you smirking about?"

Her grin widened to an all out laugh. "You. The look on your face."

Turning to stare out the window, his frown deepened. "What about my brother?" His glare should have seared the glass, and when he turned it on her, Cassie hurt.

"Why are you upset with me?" she countered. "Your brother is helping *me* to figure out what happened to *you*. Why would that bother you?"

Todd's mouth worked but no sounds came out. He slouched further. "I don't know," he muttered. "Because it's Jessie. Perfect Jessie who never did anything wrong. Who'd never do something so stupid as get himself killed."

Cassie gasped. "Todd, you aren't stupid. You know it was an accident. You didn't do this on purpose."

"So, why do I feel stupid?"

She hated to see him hurting like this. "I don't know what happened or why. All I can do is try and find out for you."

As she stared at him his shape rippled, almost as if waves of red ran through him. She sat back, a little unnerved.

"Cassie. I'm pissed," he said, his voice rising in crescendo. "As in deep, searing anger."

Feeling conspicuous, Cassie surreptitiously glanced around the room. Did no one else hear him? Apparently not. Todd spoke again.

"Can't you understand? I don't want to be dead. I want to be alive. I did not do this to myself. I feel cheated, damn it."

Fury, pain and grief radiated out from Todd. Cassie's own heart hurt for his loss, and her own. His emotions had to be much more magnified. She didn't know what to say. Everything felt inadequate. "I'm so sorry," she whispered.

He studied her face. Cassie swore she saw a glimmer of moisture in his eyes as he started to fade.

"Wait." She leaned forward. "Your funeral's on Friday."

The shimmering fade slowed, hitched, then he blinked out altogether.

Cassie lowered her head, blinking back tears.

"Cassie?"

She jerked up. "What?" And saw a face so like Todd's...with effort, she shifted gears.

"Hi. Grab a seat." She managed a small smile for him. It wasn't hard. After his brother's volatile visit, nice uncomplicated Jessie was perfect – even if he did look too much like his brother for comfort.

Jessie slid into the cracked vinyl bench across from her. He gave a searching glance around the empty room. "Nice décor. Not."

The restaurant had that sixties retro thing going on. Cassie loved it. So had Todd.

Bringing his gaze back to her, he said, "I hope I didn't interrupt something. I heard you talking to someone when I walked in."

Heat rose on her cheeks. Of course he'd have heard her. "No problem. I'm done." Searching for a new topic before she started blabbing on about his brother's ghost, she nodded to the coffee cup in hand. "Is that coffee?"

"What?" He looked down at his hand. "Oh yeah. I thought I'd try it black. The last one a friend fixed for me and it was loaded with sugar and cream."

Cassie couldn't help but grin. "Bet it was a girl."

A sheepish grin, so like Todd's slid out. "Yeah, it was. It was horrible. Like a hot milkshake without the ice cream." He gave a mock shudder.

"Black might be too strong, though," Cassie warned.

"I'll be fine." He stirred his cup, studying her face. "How are you doing? With Todd's death?"

Was he serious? "I lost my best friend. I saw Todd almost every day and spoke or texted with him dozens of times in a day. I feel lost. How do you expect me to feel?" Despite her best intentions, Cassie's voice raised, attracting attention. She groaned and slunk down. "Now look what you made me do."

Jessie just shook his head. "I'm sorry. I just…feel awkward about all this, I guess."

Cassie closed her eyes. "No. It's not your fault. I'm so touchy these days. Sorry, I shouldn't have snapped at you." She turned to stare aimlessly out the window. "In truth, sometimes it's fine and all I do is smile when I think of him. Other times I cry. And sometimes I get mad." She shrugged, still not looking at him. "No matter what anyone thought of him, nobody deserves to die at eighteen. His whole life was ahead of him."

"That's what my mom keeps saying."

"Speaking of your mom, why didn't she have more to do with Todd? He hated that. It bugged him constantly that she didn't love him."

"What?" He leaned forward, lowering his voice. "Of course, she loved him."

"Well, that's not the way he saw it. As far as he knew, you were the chosen one and he lost out." Cassie stirred her cup, studying his face. His was open, mobile. Todd's had that cynical world-weary look. They were so much the same and so different. Like all siblings, she supposed. Not that she had any to compare.

Jessie looked absolutely stunned. His mouth opened and closed several times. "Are you serious? Did he say that?"

"Yes. Several times. He was really jealous of you, you know."

"Jealous. Why? He had the freedom to do whatever he wanted. He had Dad, I didn't. Not sure I wanted to, but I couldn't help thinking they were doing father and son things I didn't know about. My mom loves me and I love her, but that's not the same thing."

Cassie considered the other half of the problem. "Why couldn't you guys share? I don't get it. There are two parents and two kids, why couldn't you spend time with both parents? You both needed a mom and a dad."

Jessie stared around the almost empty restaurant. "Mom and dad fought a lot. Then dad started to really drink and she couldn't take it anymore. Before we knew it, the situation had become 'them against us.' It's not the way Todd and I wanted it, but we soon found ourselves on opposite sides of the fence. Not enemies exactly, but neither were we friends."

"Sad."

"Yeah, especially now that he's gone and there's no longer a chance to be anything more." He lifted his cup and took the first sip. And scrunched up his face.

Cassie giggled. "It's not that bad."

He tried a second sip and this time barely winced. He nodded bravely by the time he finished. "Not bad. I can see it's growing on me."

"Good. So how do you feel about ghosts?"

He raised his head and looked at her. "What?"

"I asked how you felt about ghosts."

With a half grin, he gave a half shrug. "Not having seen any, it's hard to know what to say."

"Hmmm." Cassie wondered why Todd was only visible to her. Surely his family or other friends should be able to see him, too.

"Is this an arbitrary question or does it have something to do with my brother's death?"

Cassie grinned. "It's arbitrary. Tell me the details of the funeral."

Adam Spence hated his life. He hated the booze bottle that sat permanently attached to his hand. And he really hated the popcorn ceiling that hovered over his living room. Remnants of the seventies' era when life had been simpler, happier. Somewhere, somehow he'd lost his place in the world. Now he was haunted by his actions and lack of actions. He wanted his son back and that couldn't happen – not any more.

And he wanted his ex-wife to shut up.

She called all the time. What's with all the questions about Todd's casket or the dress code for the funeral and what flowers to have there? Like he cared. Or that Todd cared.

Then she'd asked him to quit drinking again so he could spend fatherly time with Jessie. Said he was struggling with his brother's loss and needed him. And time was too short.

The leather couch crackled under his weight as he shifted and reached for the bottle of gin. The whiskey was long gone. He took a heavy gulp, letting the firewater slide down his raw throat. There shouldn't be any membranes left to hurt, but somehow there were.

Spend quality time, she'd said. Help Jessie to grow up and be a man. Like who was she fooling? Look what had happened to Todd. Guilt speared through him. He'd been a horrible father.

If she only knew.

CHAPTER SEVEN

Yesterday Cassie had forgotten to ask Jessie to check his dad's house for Todd's cell phone. Cassie had called the number several times, but the calls went to voicemail immediately. She didn't know what that meant. She hadn't been able to let go of the possibility that Todd might not have had it on him when he'd crashed.

Cassie left for school a little earlier than usual. She appreciated the sunlight and warmth. It felt like days since she'd enjoyed a morning like this. On the way, she texted Jessie, asking him to follow up on possible locations for the missing phone.

As soon as she sent it, guilt poked her. Her coffee with Jessie had shifted something between them – brought them closer together. Only now that she'd had a chance to connect on a deeper level, he no longer seemed like Todd's brother – just a terrific guy in his own right.

Even though Jessie was helping her get answers, she felt disloyal to Todd each time she found him attractive. Only Todd wasn't here and Jessie was. And she'd always had a crush on him.

Penny had called last night, squealing when Cassie told her about the meeting. Then she'd gone quiet, asking if Cassie was trying to replace Todd, and wouldn't it be better to find someone else? Because Jessie shouldn't be looked at as a stand-in for Todd.

Cassie hadn't thought about it that way. Why would she? Todd was still here with her, and now she was becoming friends with his brother. A brother she'd wanted to spend a lot of time with before – and hadn't been able to. Sounded good to her.

As she walked the many blocks to school, she considered the couple of hours of research on the after-world that she'd managed to squeeze in between her Math and English homework last night. Her mom had come in, seen the monitor, compressed her lips and had left quickly. Cassie had been afraid that her father would bolt up the stairs to haul her computer away after that.

It wasn't like she was becoming obsessed or like a Goth or Emo type of person. They had several of those at school. Todd had been friendly with a bunch of them. That had been Todd, an all-around friendly guy. And he'd so liked the girls. And the girls had so liked him.

Cassie wondered what Todd's future would have been like if he hadn't died. He'd have graduated in less than two months, and then what? Todd never did answer her question about whether he'd applied to college or not. He'd just laughed and said he had loads of time.

How wrong could one be?

And what did she want to do herself? She couldn't help wonder about her own future. Become a veterinarian? Go into biological, or even environmental science?

It seemed too far away for her to care and yet, for Todd, the end had come so early – at least the end of one kind of existence.

According to her research, there've been thousands of ghost sightings, with the ghosts usually hanging around because of unfinished business. In Todd's case, she assumed the unanswered questions regarding his death kept him here. And when he found his answers, he'd leave.

Her heart constricted, and for a second she struggled for breath. If just the thought of his leaving hurt her like that, how was she going to handle it when that time actually came? She knew the only reason she was 'handling' his death was because to her he wasn't really gone. But when he truly was…

Determined to throw off that depressing line of thought, Cassie stopped to admire a beautiful garden where thousands of white flowers cascaded over a stone wall. Stunning. This life had so much beauty, so much to offer; she understood someone wanting to stay after their death. If they had a choice.

Earthbound is the explanation she'd found in her research. Immediately her mind conjured up images of Todd wrapped like a mummy in white bandages and caught on a bush in the forest. So not the image Heartthrob Todd would want to be remembered by.

"Well, well, if it isn't little Miss Perfect."

Cassie rolled her eyes as four of Todd's friends caught up to her. She walked faster. She had only a block to go to meet her friends. These druggies weren't her friends. They were heavy drinkers and hung around the back of the school and did drugs during the day, their lives already set on a destructive path.

"What's the matter, Little Prissy? Too good for us now that Todd's not here? Or just scared because he's not here to protect you?"

Protect? Had Todd kept these lowlifes away from her? If he had, she owed him more than she'd known. "I don't need protection. You guys will just crawl back under your rocks soon anyway. After all, it's daylight and that's sleepy time for the creepy crawlers."

"Hey, what did she just say to us?"

Cassie grinned. Aric was big and burly but didn't know what end was up on any given day. Definitely a dunce – a relatively harmless one. "I said I'll see you at Todd's funeral. I'm sure that as his friends you'll all show up and pay your respects." She dashed up the front steps of the school, relieved to see Penny and Suzie waiting in front of the double doors, their smiles a bright beacon. Linking arms, she tugged both girls through the doors. "Are they still following me?"

"No, they never came up the stairs. Were they hassling you?"

"Yeah, something about Todd not being here to protect me."

Penny turned to look behind them, searching for the teens. "They're gone."

"Figures."

"What did they want?"

"I don't know."

But it did make her wonder. Had one of them been with Todd when he died? If they'd called Todd for a ride that night, he'd have gone to pick them up. He'd done that so many times before.

"It might explain their comments this morning," she muttered under her breath. She'd have to mention that to the deputy when they met again this afternoon. Then she remembered her parents. They didn't want her to talk about Todd's death. And wouldn't appreciate her taking a second trip to the sheriff's office. She pondered the issue throughout the afternoon. She could hardly rope Jessie into doing this too.

Still, someone had been in that vehicle with Todd. It was the only viable explanation, at least for her. But how to find out?

All around her, students worked quietly on their assignments. She studied their bent heads. What about Todd's online presence? Was anyone looking after that? Her cell phone plan was only basic and had no Internet. Much to her disgust.

At the sound of the school bell, Cassie raced home, saying a quick, 'hi,' to her mom before taking the stairs two at a time and opening her laptop. Booting up the laptop, she quickly accessed her account. *Geesh*. She'd posted about having a personal loss and that she'd be offline for a couple of days. She hadn't thought to check Todd's pages.

There. Someone had created a memorial page. She frowned, feeling both guilty and pissed. She was Todd's best friend. She should have done this for him.

She read the wall and the multitude of comments. Though most were friendly, some were not. She tried to ignore those, although some were particularly difficult to read. Trying to hold the anger back she scrolled down the many entries. Opening another window she ran through the Twitter feeds...same old, same old.

What if she posted something to stir things up? Something about hoping that the people riding in the vehicle with Todd on the night he was killed would turn themselves in. Or would that get her in more trouble?

It was her call, yet she didn't want to do something stupid. So no then. Chewing on her bottom lip, she went to the school website and checked if they'd posted a notice. There was a small corner article dedicated to Todd's memory, mentioning the time and location of the funeral. A note stated grief counselors were available to speak with any student who needed to talk. Cassie slumped back, rubbing her hands over her eyes. Should she talk to someone? Doubt worried away at her.

Was she losing it? Was she imagining Todd's ghost? She had to wonder. No one else could see him. Maybe only people who cared could see him, but then what about Todd's mother? She loved him. Only Todd hadn't believed that. So maybe he could only be seen by people he felt loved him. That probably limited the list to her.

How sad.

If Cassie died, who could she visit? Her mom and dad? Maybe. Possibly Penny and Suzie. Grams and Todd, if they'd been alive. Her eyes narrowed. Maybe there were only a few special people for everyone.

Cassie stood up, unable to drop the idea of posting something on Facebook. Would they have to know the post was from her? Could she create a different account and post that way? Could she post anonymously? Or did that not work?

She couldn't check Todd's email. He'd never given her his password. She hadn't really wanted it. He had a lot of correspondence with his girlfriends that she so didn't want to see. Yuck.

What about Todd's laptop? Where was it now and had anyone checked it over for clues?

And who had created the memorial page?

***

Todd leaned against the pantry door in his mom's kitchen. How many times had he visited here since his parents divorced? Six, seven times. Maybe more at the beginning. In the last two years maybe once. By then he'd felt like an outsider.

Right now she was at the stove cooking. Todd sniffed the air, before remembering that he had no sense of smell. He paused. Was that garlic? He frowned. There was a faint smell. Spaghetti? Sights were brighter on this side. Then there were times where everything was flat, one dimensional. He didn't know what made it one way or the other. He'd seen other people like him wandering around, but he couldn't communicate with them.

It was horribly confusing...and lonely. Thank heavens for Cassie. She was the only one he missed. The only person he'd cared about. Sure, he had girlfriends. They were girls for fun not for friendship. Cassie was different. He'd never kissed her – well, not a real kiss. He'd dropped kisses on her cheeks, maybe even on her lips, except they weren't *those* kinds of kisses. He wanted her to be happy. But he'd rather it be with him and not his brother.

Just then, Jessie walked into the room, texting someone. Todd walked up behind him trying to see who he was messaging. Cassie.

He twisted his head, trying to read the message and missed it.

"Jessie, set the table, please."

"Sure, Mom." Todd followed every footstep his brother took. He actually tried to breathe down his brother's neck, hoping for some acknowledgment that of his presence. Nothing.

Todd felt like he was in a horror flick. Waiting for the killer to jump out from behind the cupboard. A killer only he could see.

He hated this. He'd chosen not to interact with these people when he'd been alive. He'd figured it didn't matter. They didn't matter.

He'd been wrong.

"Jessie, no cell phones at the table."

Jessie grimaced, checked the message and shoved it away again. "Sorry." He polished off the spaghetti on his plate, then carried it over to the sink and washed his dishes. "I'm off to do my homework." Taking the stairs two at a time, he raced to his room.

Todd followed. Jessie had been a little too fast on that exit. In his room, Jessie pulled out his phone and made a call. "Cassie, yeah. I know. I searched. There's no sign of it. I asked my mom if the cell phone was in Todd's personal effects, she said she didn't know."

Todd jumped closer to hear Cassie's answers. He couldn't.

"I don't know that she's even looked. She's been to the sheriff's office and to the funeral home. We have to go back on Friday, with the clothes he's to wear for the burial. It's possible my dad has the stuff, however there's also no guarantee that he's looked either. Or that there was a cell phone in with the rest. Whatever the rest is."

"I know there should be his wallet and that necklace you gave him for his birthday." Jessie nodded. "Yeah, I'll try Dad's place next."

Stepping back, Todd stumbled around the room, slightly disoriented. Jessie was helping Cassie? Really? To find out what had happened to him?

He hadn't seen that one coming. Sure, Cassie had mentioned it, only he hadn't believed Jessie would. The concept rolled around his head. Nothing bad or good came to mind. He didn't know how he felt about it. If he were still alive, it would piss him off to see them together, but now, well, maybe that would be good for both of them.

He sighed. Being dead was very confusing.

***

Cassie put the phone down. Who took home the personal effects in a case like this? The mom or the dad? Did the dad have actual custody of Todd, if so he'd be the one to get them, wouldn't he? If they shared custody and the mom was making the funeral arrangements, she'd be the one most likely to take them. Cassie needed to find out what happened to the cell phone. It might be nothing or it could provide all the answers.

Should she contact the deputy and ask him? She opened up a web page and searched for the contact information. There. St. Paul's County Sherriff's Office. There were phone numbers and a map. No email addresses. Well, there was, but only for the main office reception. She checked the directory. Bingo. The deputy's email address was there.

She opened her email account, then jotted down a draft email, trying to list the questions that sat uppermost on her mind. The cell phone was the biggest issue. Plus she wanted to know if the deputy had found any new information. Not that he'd tell her what it was. Still, she mentioned the people Todd had been with that last night, just on the off chance he hadn't already followed up.

She sat back and reread what she'd written. She chewed uncertainly on the inside of her lips. Should she mention Todd's friends who'd accosted her on the way to school? Could Todd have been partying with any of those kids?

She finished with a quick apology for taking up so much time and that she just really needed to know that everything possible had been done to find the truth. She hit send then sat back and said, to the empty room, "There's really not much more I can do."

"And that's already plenty. Thank you."

"Todd," she spun around with a happy grin on her face. "Wow. It's good to see you. I never know if or when you're going to show again. Each visit is a gift, as it could be the last time."

He grinned. "Yeah, for me, too."

She laughed, shaking her head. "You're such an idiot."

"What?" he protested. "You know I love being able to spend time with you like this."

"What's it like?" She tilted her head. "Do you get tired? Sleep? Do you eat? Or do you want to eat?" She studied his face. "Do you get cold?"

"Whoa." Laughing, Todd strode over to her bed and sat down comfortably against the pillows. Except there was no indentation where he lay.

Cassie shook her head. This stuff was pretty wild. "So...answer."

Holding up one hand, Todd laughed as he counted the questions off. "No, I don't get cold. No, I haven't found myself tired yet. I'd love to eat, but don't think I can as I can't pick up anything to begin with. However, I'm never hungry, so it doesn't matter."

Cassie thought about his answers. "How are you doing inside? Still angry or starting to get over it?"

"Not even beginning to get over it. I don't want to be dead, Cassie. As much as I hated school, I'd give anything to be able to go there again."

His lopsided grin was tinged with sadness. "Too bad kids can't spend a day playing 'dead' to learn to appreciate what they have."

Sobering thought. Cassie asked curiously, "What would you change? You know, *if* you could come back?"

"I'd definitely want to get to know my mom and my brother better. Drop the multitude of girlfriends and buddies and work to find more true friends." He stared up at the ceiling. "Regrets are the worst. People I didn't appreciate, like Mom. Things I wish I'd done more of, like riding my motorcycle, fishing,

snowboarding. And spending time with people I care about –
like you."

Tears threatened to fall. Cassie brushed them away and
sniffled. "We have this time now."

"Right." He sat up, swung his legs over the side of the bed
and asked. "What have you found out?"

She brought him up to date. "Finding the cell phone would
be a huge plus. With it I could figure out if someone called and
asked for a ride home that night. Or maybe someone sent you on
an errand after you dropped the others off."

He frowned down at his clasped hands. "I can't remember
the last time I used it. I remember taking Ivan to his house and
then turning toward home." He shook his head. "The rest is still
a blank."

"I wonder if those memories are accessible."

Todd looked at her in horror. "There's no way I'm going to
let you play around inside my mind, so forget that idea."

Cassie couldn't resist a bit of dark humor. "Why not?
What's the worst thing that could happen? You're already dead!"

His grin was pure devil. "But you're not – yet!"

She laughed.

"Cassie?"

Her door pushed open. Her mother stood the doorway, one
hand on the door knob. "Who are you talking to, honey?"

Cassie groaned silently. Quick. What could she say to her
mom? "Hi, Mom, did you want something?" Cassie cast a quick
glance over at the bed. As she'd suspected Todd had stretched
back out on the coverlet with a big grin on his face.

Her mom frowned, her eyes darting around the room
before returning to Cassie's face; a confused frown furrowed her
forehead.

"I thought I heard voices?"

"Probably the computer. I was playing a bunch of YouTube
videos."

"Oh." Abby didn't appear to know what to say to that. She looked uncertain for another moment before awkwardly backing out. "Maybe turn the volume down, so it's not quite so disturbing."

Cassie tossed her a carefree smile. "Sure, Mom, no problem."

She watched as the door shut, then tilted her head to listen to her mother's retreating footsteps. Only then did she turn back to the still grinning Todd. She held her finger up to her lips.

Todd laughed. "It's not me you need to worry about."

Cassie rolled her eyes. "I know. I can't seem to remember to keep my voice down around you. When you show up in public places, I come off looking like a mental case."

"No problem. That's a normal state for you."

On impulse, Cassie threw her pen at him. And watched in awe as it slipped right through Todd and fell onto the coverlet. She'd go nuts thinking about this stuff. Keeping her voice down, she asked, "Would you have seen those druggie friends of yours on Friday night?"

Todd sat up again, his face a confused puzzle. "What do you mean?"

"Could they have called you to come and join them somewhere? Or asked you to pick them up? Or do a delivery for them?" Frustrated, she threw out her hands. "Someone you know had to be in that car with you. Unless you picked up a hitchhiker?"

His brows veered together. "I don't pick up hitchhikers unless I know them."

"Maybe you picked up one you knew? Your vehicle went off Pinnacle Point. A mile or so away from your house."

He frowned, swinging his legs over the side, facing her. "I know it well. I always slow down, particularly when I'm coming from the North. It's got a brutal hook from that direction."

"That's where your car went over." She paused, considering. "I'd like to go see it." She stood up and stepped over to the window. "I could walk there after school tomorrow or maybe on the weekend. Maybe Jessie would come with me."

"Him?" he spat. "Why him?"

Startled, Cassie spun around to stare at him. "Because I don't have any male friends but you. And it creeps me out to think of going there alone, that's why?"

"I can go with you." He strode over to where she stood, reaching out to grab her shoulders.

She glanced down at his hands, sinking into her shirt. So, soft and gentle, like a fairy's stroke. Yet she felt it. She was in awe of the sensation.

"I can feel your hand." She lifted her arm, her fingers, gentle and soothing stroked down the side of his cheekbone. Those clear emerald eyes, so intent and sharp, glowed. His eyelids drifted closed at her touch, his head tilting, disappearing into her palm.

Tears came to Cassie's eyes.

"Why did this have to happen to you?" she whispered.

He opened his eyes. "I don't know. And I don't know how long I can stay here. Things are starting to fade. It's getting harder to communicate sometimes."

Cassie's lower lip trembled. "But I..."

"Shh." He lifted one finger, gently stroking along the plump line of her mouth. "It's okay. I'm getting used to this. I'll be alright."

"Yeah, and what about me?"

A sad look slid over his face. "You will be fine too. You'll miss me, and I'm grateful someone will." As she made to speak, he placed a finger against her mouth. "No. I know how things stand. There's nothing like having lots of time on your hands, being able to travel anywhere at any time and listening to conversations without people being aware...to get a good idea of how they truly felt about you."

Turning her head away, Cassie closed her eyes at the thought. She whispered, "I imagine that's a little difficult."

"Let's say it gives one a unique perspective on human dynamics."

"Too bad we can't have that perspective without dying first," she said bitterly.

"We could, only most of us can't be bothered to do anything as constructive as being the best we can be." A mocking laugh escaped. "We'd much rather do for ourselves than for others."

His beloved features faded, before dissipating altogether in front of her.

Tears sprang to her eyes as he vanished. She should have asked him some more questions. Questions about the conversations he might have heard. People talked. And the one who been in his vehicle would say something to someone someday.

Todd had sounded so different at the end. So…mature. As if dying had hurt in ways unimaginable. And his experience was so different from hers, she didn't know what to say, what to think. He was expanding her world with every sentence, and she had no time to absorb everything. No time to process. No time to re-evaluate her beliefs about life and death – and that place somewhere in-between.

Where Todd existed.

CHAPTER EIGHT

Ten minutes after last bell, Jessie slouched against the school gates, waiting for Cassie. She'd called at lunch with an odd request.

He wasn't keen on going to the crash site. Still, he wouldn't let her go alone. True, she was obsessing over the missing phone, but he understood her determination. He respected it.

Todd had been lucky to have her as a friend.

"Hi, Jessie. Thanks for coming with me." She stood before him, a vision in yellow. Her hair bounced in a high ponytail held together by a yellow clip that matched her bright t-shirt. Fresh and pretty as spring flowers, she pleased him in ways he'd never known before.

Straightening, he gave her a goofy grin. "No problem. Let's go, though. I have a ton of homework."

They fell into step and turned toward the Shake Shop.

"I do, too. I figured we could grab a coffee on the way." When Jessie's face scrunched, she smirked. "My treat."

His sidelong glance made her laugh out loud. "It's not that bad, surely?"

"Right."

They picked up coffees, then headed to Pinnacle Point, just out of town. The traffic was steady. However with a wide shoulder they weren't bothered. Fifteen minutes later they could see the turn up ahead, with all its warning signs in bright yellow. Cassie's footsteps slowed at the sharp reality. Jessie stopped at her side.

"Rough corner."

"No kidding." The pavement had black skid marks going around the bend in both directions. The gravel was scuffed up and there were distinct tracks heading off the highway. Silence fell between Cassie and Jessie. What was there to say? This is where his brother had driven off the highway to crash below. The gas had leaked and supposedly, within a short time, the vehicle had been engulfed in flames.

Todd had been found many yards up the hill, dead.

***

Cassie stood at the corner, staring down at the horrific skid marks, scattered metal pieces and charred marks centered on one huge black spot. Shivers settled in on her spine and wouldn't stop. She pulled her sweater out of her backpack and put it on. Her heart sank. *Poor Todd.*

With a quick sideways look at Jessie, Cassie noted his grim features before turning her attention to the accident site below.

Todd stood below her, waving wildly at her, a big grin on his face. Cassie turned to Jessie. "I'm going down."

"What?" He glanced around to see if anyone might bother them. The highway was empty. "Are you sure you want to?"

"I'm here. I might as well."

The hill had a surprisingly steep slope. She couldn't imagine what it had been like inside a car smashing over and over again. *Here goes nothing.* Cassie started down, only to have Jessie pass her with his first jump. Half-sliding, half-skidding, they made it down to where the car had come to its final resting place. The car had been hauled away. Still skid marks, a large burned area and a mess of footprints that had churned the soil up, easily pointing to the spot.

At the bottom, Cassie smiled at Todd, after a quick look in Jessie's direction. She managed to keep her mouth shut. Jessie would freak if he knew. She wandered around trying to decipher the mess left behind from the recovery operations. There were scorch marks and burnt shrubs making it easy to see where the vehicle had been, but where had Todd dragged himself to?

"Cassie, what are you looking for?"

She didn't know, just knew she'd recognize it when she saw it. Cassie had the presence of mind to check who was speaking before answering. "I don't know, Jessie. Anything. Something to help determine if a second person had been in the vehicle."

Todd walked over. "There's nothing here. Or too much; look at the footprints. Looks like a freakin' party happened." Todd wandered around the same area as Cassie. "I don't feel any connection to this place. I don't get it." Moodily, he kicked at a rock and hissed when his foot went through it.

Wanting to answer him, and not knowing how to with Jessie around, Cassie could only give him a commiserating look and keep an eye on Jessie. She needn't have worried as Jessie wandered around the far side of the site. Cassie widened her search, heading around the brush and trees. "Todd," she whispered. "At least try to help. Search for your cell phone. That's why we're here."

"Hey! What are you two doing down there?" A strange voice hailed them from the top of the embankment.

"Uh, oh. Now you've done it." Todd smirked at Cassie.

She shot him a dirty look before holding a hand to her eyes to block the sun so she could see who spoke. The sun was still too bright for her to see the speaker. "Nothing. Just looking for a friend's cell phone."

"That's not a good place to be right now. Didn't you hear a kid died down there a few days ago?"

Cassie glanced at Jessie, who only shrugged. "We're on our way up."

With Cassie leading the way, they struggled back up the side of the hill. The old timer was still there. Cassie gasped for breath as she glanced around. An occasional vehicle passed, but there was no sign of this guy's vehicle. She studied the scrawny senior citizen in front of her. Mid-seventies, gaunt. Suspenders held up his pants, and his long sleeved shirt was clean and buttoned to the neck. She smiled at him. "Are you walking, too?"

"What? No, I live up there." He pointed to a barely visible rooftop in the trees on the opposite side of the road.

"Really?" Cassie studied the hidden location. "Wow. I've lived here all my life and never knew that place existed." Even now that she knew, it was hard to pick out the house. If he hadn't pointed it out, she'd never have seen it. There was a driveway of some kind, but it was half hidden in the bushes. "I guess this is a bad corner for accidents, huh?"

The old man rubbed a hand over his thin head of hair. "Terrible. That boy's was something awful to see. I called for help right away. The last thing we needed was to have that fire take off. If it hadn't been for the heavy rain these last few days, it would have burned down quite a patch. "

"Did you see what happened?" Jessie asked curiously, stuffing his fists into his jean pockets. His mannerisms were so like Todd's, Cassie had to turn away. She searched the area for Todd, but there was no sign of him.

Turning her attention back to the conversation, Cassie watched the two men interact. One old, with a weather-lined face, probably from having seen so much he'd like to forget and Jessie, so young he couldn't imagine what the other had forgotten.

"Like how it happened? Nope. Not that I saw it exactly. I heard it, then saw all that fire. It had to have been over quick."

"Yes, except the boy managed to get out of the vehicle. He never was injured by the fire." Cassie studied his wrinkled face, hoping he'd remember something.

"Is that right?" He hitched up his faded jeans, tucking his plaid shirt in as he looked down at the burn area. "Figured he'd have been burned to a crisp by the time the police got there."

Cassie couldn't resist asking, "Did you see him moving around at all? Getting out of the vehicle? Or anyone crawling up the hill? Voices? Anything? We'd like to find out if Todd was alone, or if he had someone in the vehicle with him."

The old man directed his sharp blue eyes at her, before saying in a slow, thoughtful way, "Ain't that for the police to figure out?"

Cassie looked at Jessie and both turned to face the stranger. "They've decided he was drinking and driving and was alone in the vehicle. Todd was Jessie's brother and my best friend." She lifted her chin. "He didn't drink and drive."

The stranger studied them. "Well, I can see as you might be a tad upset about their ruling. Did you speak to them about it?"

"We both have, actually. They were going to get back to us on a few questions that we raised. Like where's Todd's cell phone?"

"You thinking he called someone?"

The sun came out from behind a cloud. Cassie rubbed her temple, wishing she'd remembered to bring her sunglasses. "He often picked up friends who had been drinking and gave them rides home."

"Still, he'd have been behind the wheel, right?"

After a moment, Cassie nodded reluctantly. "Probably. He loved that car. It was his first one."

At that the old man rubbed a hand along the side of his cheek, pondering her words. "Well, I could ask Martha, I suppose. She stayed outside to keep an eye on the fire while I went to call the police."

"Oh. That would be great! It would make us feel so much better if we knew the truth."

"It can't do any harm. That Martha, she's got the eyes of hawk, she has. But she's resting right now and I won't be waking her for this."

"No, not necessary." Cassie fished around in her purse, looking for a piece of paper, when Jessie held a small notepad under her nose.

"Use this."

With a grateful smile, she snagged up one of the half-dozen pens lying at the bottom on her purse and wrote down both their names and numbers. "After you talk to her, would you contact one of us and let us know what she says?"

He read off the names and nodded. "I reckon I can do that." Spearing them with sharp blue eyes, he added, "It might not be tonight, you know. Martha's in a bad way and has been known to sleep for a long time sometimes."

Jessie smiled. "No problem, sir. Tomorrow or the day after would be fine. My brother's funeral is tomorrow."

"Is it now? Well, you give that young man a good send-off. It's too bad he's gone so young, however, we can't have everyone thinking he'd done something he didn't do, now can we – not if there's another explanation."

"No, we can't. Thank you so much." Cassie smiled brilliantly at him. "We really appreciate it."

They waved good-bye and started down the long road into town.

CHAPTER NINE

Friday was a crappy day to be buried on. Okay, so it's not like there was a good day but everyone hates Mondays, so why not then? On the other hand, Todd had loved Fridays. Maybe he'd appreciate this choice.

Cassie didn't. The whole concept depressed her and would most likely ruin her whole weekend. She'd wanted Penny to come with her, only she couldn't get out of her shift at work. She'd asked Suzie. Suzie's excuse was that she detested funerals and graveyards and that 'whole dead thing,' as she put it. Jessie would attend with his family. She'd called Ivan and Bryce, but they'd already left for the ceremony.

That meant Cassie had to go alone. She'd thought about asking her mom to go with her but had vetoed that idea pretty fast. Her mom hadn't liked Todd. She wouldn't insult her best friend by bringing people who hadn't appreciated him. Their loss, not his. So Cassie found black jeans in the back of the closet and paired them with a navy t-shirt and a black pullover.

Thankfully, the forecast for rain had turned out to be wrong and the sun had chosen to bless the day. Afraid of being late, she took the back way into the cemetery and joined the small group surrounding a simple raised wooden casket. Todd stood beside Jessie, a mocking grin on his face as he watched the proceedings.

Cassie beamed at him and gave him a little wave, only to blink in horror as people turned to stare. She stuffed her hand in her pocket and tried to hide amongst the gatherers. Looking around, she hated that less than two-dozen people had attended, and that included the family, the minister and Todd. She recognized the school principal and several teachers. That made her grin. She figured Todd would appreciate the humor that his teachers showed up for his funeral, when he hadn't bothered to show up for their classes.

"A perfect day for a perfect service, don't you think?" Todd appeared beside her, making her jump. Cassie shuffled to give him room only to belatedly realize he didn't need any, having squeezed in, between her and another person. She glared at him, wanting to punch him, only not wanting to draw attention to herself. She rolled her eyes at him instead. He was so juvenile sometimes.

Noticing the strange look at her from another student, Cassie stared forward and concentrated on the proceedings. The ceremony took so little time, she didn't notice it was over until the casket was lowered and Jessie and his mom threw dirt on top on top of it.

Where was Todd's father? There, in a rumpled suit, his nose red and bulbous. He followed behind his ex-wife and son.

Cassie waited until most of the crowd had dispersed before standing at the end of the grave. She'd only ever attended Grams' funeral, which had been a church service and not a service beside an open gravesite. She figured Todd would prefer this one.

"Oh, Todd." Pressure built up inside. She hated crying in public but figured that funerals might be the one place where it was allowed. She sniffled and sighed. "Damn it, Todd, why did you go and get yourself killed?"

"Like it's my fault now, huh?"

She glanced sideways to see that killer grin of his. As he stared down at his own coffin the grin fell away. "Makes it a little too real, doesn't it?"

"Yeah," she whispered. "Then having you stand there as a ghost is fairly disturbing, too."

"You know me, always gotta have some drama in my life."

She smiled. A little watery, but it was a smile. Resolutely she turned and walked away. Several cars and a limousine stood at the cemetery gate. By coming through the back, she'd missed seeing everyone arrive. Jessie stood beside his parents, speaking with the principal.

"Cassie, come on over here." Principal Macintosh called to her, a concerned look on his face. "How are you doing?"

She gave him a wan smile, hoping the redness on her face had calmed down. "I'm okay. It's a tough day for all of us."

"It is that." He motioned toward the people beside him. "Do you know Todd's mother and his brother?"

"I know Jessie," she interrupted, smiling gently at Todd's mother. "Hello, Mrs. Spence. I'm so sorry about Todd. He was my best friend, and I couldn't have asked for a better one."

Tears collected in the older woman's eyes. She blinked several times before speaking. "Thank you for saying that, Cassie. I wish I'd known him as well as you did. Unfortunately, these last few years, well, we'd grown apart."

"Really, is that what you call it?"

Cassie's eyes widened as she realized Todd was standing between them, staring at his mother.

"She could have tried harder, you know." Todd turned to look at Cassie, a frown on his face. "I'll take some of the blame, except she has to take some of it, too."

It was hard to focus on what Mrs. Spence was saying when Todd was being so difficult. She turned slightly so he wasn't in her line of focus. Directing her voice at Todd's mother, Cassie said, "I'm sure Todd loved you regardless of how far you might have drifted lately. There's a strong bond between mother and son."

A watery smile peeped out. "Thanks. And thank you for being such a good friend to him. He cared for you. He did share that much."

Cassie tried not to look at Todd, who'd decided to be a major ass. Was he really doing the chicken dance? Forcing her attention back to his mom, she said, "Thank you. I'm just sorry he's gone. He was way too young to die. He had such plans for his future." Cassie's heart lightened at the memory of Todd's dreams. "He wanted to travel, and try bungee jumping and planned on windsurfing in Canada." Her smile dimmed slightly. "Todd was a good person. Given a chance, he'd have made you proud. I miss him terribly."

Cassie gave the group a small wave, tears burning in her eyes. "Now if you'll excuse me, I'm going to head home. Today has been difficult."

"For all of us." Mrs. Spence reached over and gave her a quick hug. "Thank you so much for coming."

"Thanks, Cassie." Jessie opened the door and helped his mom get into the limo. "I'll see you at school on Monday."

Cassie nodded, offering a small smile just for him. "Sure. If you want to get out, go for a walk, have coffee or something on the weekend, just give me a call."

***

Jessie watched Cassie stride away. Alone. He'd never admired her more. She'd lost as much as the rest of them, maybe even more. Yet she'd come alone - without anyone to support her. Regardless of being dressed in black like the rest of them, Cassie would never blend into a crowd. Her blond hair bounced with the very vitality of her step. Although, she looked skinnier.

"Jessie?"

Startled, he turned to find his mother staring at him, a curious look on her face as she peered out at him from deep inside the limousine. "Aren't you getting in?"

Jessie shook off his reverie. Cassie would have to wait. As much as he'd like to walk her home and make sure she was alright, his mother needed him more. She always did. Today it was understandable. Jessie was all she had left.

Had Todd felt that way about Dad?

Always feeling like the adult of the house? Watching as the adults degenerated further into dependency?

Jessie took his seat inside the limousine and wondered at the showiness of driving to a funeral in such a vehicle. It all seemed so ostentatious. For his mother, it was the 'right' thing to do. Todd wouldn't have cared one bit.

He was coming to realize funerals weren't for the dead, but for the living that the dead left behind.

***

Saturday dawned ugly and cold. May showers. Cassie huddled under her covers. She had no plans for the weekend. To make matters worse, it was housework day - again. Still, having something to do was better than being left alone with her thoughts. She'd never let her mother know that though. Groaning, she rolled over and closed her eyes. It wasn't worth getting out of bed yet.

When she woke up the second time, hours had passed. Cassie still felt like crap. She shivered as she rose from bed and headed to the shower. It was going to take a lot for her to enjoy this day. Getting dressed, she heard the doorbell, followed by voices. Company? On a Saturday? Great.

Maybe she could slip out to the mall, meet up with the girls. Shopping for something nice and pretty might make her feel better. After the funeral, she'd holed up in her room for the evening, hoping Todd would visit, only he hadn't shown up and Cassie had gone to bed tired and teary.

Now for a new day. Cassie headed down to the kitchen and put a couple of pieces of bread in the toaster. She'd missed too many meals this last week. Her appetite had been nonexistent. She had lived on the comfort of coffee instead.

She stared at the empty coffeepot and sighed. They'd drunk it all. Served her right for getting up so late.

"Cassie, we're in the living room. Would you join us, please?"

Cassie stared at the ceiling. "Just a minute." As her toast finished, she fixed a plate, poured a glass of orange juice and walked into the living room. A strange woman sat with her parents.

"Ah, there you are. Cassie. This is Dr. Sanchez."

Cassie smiled at her. "Hello." She took a bite of her toast.

"Please sit down with us, Cassie."

Cassie raised an eyebrow and sat in the armchair in front of her. She took a drink of her orange juice and another bite of toast, waiting for someone to explain what was going on. The toast was amazingly tasty today. Her poor stomach was probably thrilled at having solid food for a change.

"Cassie…" her mother started, only to stop as if uncertain as to what to say.

Now what? Cassie sat quietly, waiting, watching as all the adults exchanged wary glances. She really wanted to sigh heavily, her trademark I'm-hard-done-by mannerism cultivated over the years, but the toast occupied her attention just fine. She took another big bite and chewed happily.

"You seem to be enjoying that piece of toast. Hungry?"

Cassie stopped chewing mid-bite and studied the stranger. "Yes."

The doctor smiled and nodded. "A healthy appetite is a good sign."

The toast didn't look quite so appetizing. "A good sign of what?" Cassie tilted her head. Come to think of it, this woman didn't look like any of her mother's friends. She wore a sturdy navy blue suit jacket and skirt and a pale blue shirt with matching navy pumps. Cassie would never get caught dead dressed like that. Too professional. Too buttoned down. Too official. The toast in her stomach started to turn somersaults. *A shrink.*

"It's a good sign that you're on the recovery from a deep shock."

Cassie very carefully put the piece of toast down on her plate. "So much for my appetite."

"Now Cassie," started Abby, leaning forward.

Cassie's father put a restraining arm on her mother's shoulder. "Cassie, you are going to see Dr. Sanchez for a while."

Abby turned slightly, frowning at him. "Tom, we aren't forcing her into this."

"The hell we aren't," muttered Tom, glaring at the three females staring back at him. "What? It needed to be said. You will all talk forever and get nowhere?"

Abby smiled gently. "But where we get to in the end is easier on all of us."

"Hmmph." He turned his glare to the window and ignored them.

Cassie's toast took on a nasty appearance. She put the plate down on the coffee table before turning to face the adults. Why did they always have to blindside her like this? It made her so mad. Couldn't they just talk to her? "And why would I be seeing Dr. Sanchez?"

Abby took a deep breath. "Honey, you're struggling with Todd's death. Dr. Sanchez can help you deal with the loss."

Cassie shook her head. "If I didn't want to speak with the grief counselors at the school why would I want to speak to Dr. Sanchez?" She glanced over at the doctor, who watched the interchange quietly. "No offense, Doctor."

Dr. Sanchez smiled, warmth and understanding softening the professional look on her face. "None taken, Cassie."

"Mom, I could have used her assistance when Grams died. I don't need it now."

Abby tilted her head to stare at her daughter. "You had a hard time when Grams passed? Why? She was old. She'd had a good life. It was her time to die."

Cassie stared at her mom. "You just don't get it, do you? Why do you think I don't ever talk to you? It's like dialing a phone number but reaching a stove instead."

Her mom's mouth opened and closed several times. She blinked, turned to look at her husband before they both turned to stare at Cassie. Cassie rolled her eyes.

With a small smile, Dr. Sanchez interrupted. "I think she means you're talking a different language."

Abby glanced between the doctor and Cassie, a question in her eyes.

"Ya think?" Cassie could hardly keep her sarcasm in control. "What do any those factors about Grams have to do with how I felt about her death? Grams was everything to me. I loved her so much. Her death crippled me. And you...you didn't even seem to care."

"What?" Abby shoved her hand to her mouth. "How can you say that? She was my mother."

"So, you're mine."

Rude; yes. Brutal; maybe. Still it felt good to finally let her mother know how she felt. Grams' death had hurt, but her parents' lack of reaction had been a betrayal at the deepest level.

Abby pulled her lips in as if she'd sucked on a lemon.

Her father stepped in. "That wasn't necessary, Cassie. You apologize to your mother, right now."

Cassie muttered, "Sorry." Then she glared at the three adults in the room. "Of course, you *know* what's best for me, don't you? Don't bother asking me what I need. Typical."

She stood up, picked up her plate and stormed in the direction of the kitchen.

Her father yelled, "Cassie, get back here. This matter isn't resolved."

"What's to resolve? You've got something you're going to force me to do, because you're the all-knowing adults, and I'm the stupid teen who has no choices." She snorted. "I have to do this or I'll get grounded for the rest of my life and won't be able to see my friends and any other horrible things you try to dream up in your all-knowing wisdom. Or I move out. Something I can't do yet." She turned and glared at the adults. "But I don't want to do this. So congratulations on *not* getting my cooperation. Oh, and I will *not* see her here. There's no way I'll speak to her while there's any chance of you two listening in." She couldn't hold back the bitterness streaming through her voice.

She spun on her heels and headed into the kitchen, her appetite long gone.

In the background she heard her mother sobbing quietly and her father blustering about *that* girl.

Cassie returned to her bedroom, grabbed her phone and purse then slipped out the back door.

Like hell she was going to do housework now.

Todd sat in the living room Cassie had stormed out of, wondering why adults never gave teenagers any credit. He wished he could materialize in front of them and tell them how special Cassie is and what a good kid she was. They would probably have a heart attack and lose consciousness before he could get the words out. Still, someone needed to give them the what for.

"I don't understand what's happened to her. She used to be so easy going and loving. Now it's like she all anger and angst." Abby sniffled into her sleeve.

"You've been too easy on her. We should have killed the relationship with Todd years ago. Well before they became 'best friends.'" He glared at the doctor. "Whatever that term means these days."

The doctor's calm never shifted. Her voice deepened slightly, a soothing tone entering. "Cassie sounds like a normal teenager. She's lost someone important and she's angry about it. On top of that, she doesn't feel there's anyone left who understands her."

"But I do. That's the thing. She won't talk to me. We used to be so close. She turned away from me after my mother passed away. It was a doubly hard time for me, as I lost my mother and daughter at the same time."

"That was a difficult time for everyone. For you and for her, since she was apparently very close to her grandmother. You can't blame yourself. At the same time, if you didn't show any sign of loss, she'd feel betrayed by your lack of emotion. As if you hadn't cared for her grandmother and she had. That betrayal would fester and almost become anger…at its worst, it almost becomes hatred."

Whew! A doctor who actually understood. This was amazing. Todd settled back to get a lesson in family psychology. Something else he wished he'd taken the time to understand better when he'd had the chance.

Cassie's father stomped to his feet and paced around the small room. "Almost – nothing! She did hate us. Still does, I'd say. At the time, she treated Abby like a pariah. It took a long time for Cassie to be civil again."

The doctor smiled as if Cassie's father said something incredibly intelligent. "That's classic textbook. Cassie's had a tough time. With the loss of her grandmother, she was forced to cope. Those same skills are helping her right now. This isn't an easy time, but she's doing the best she can. Her friend has only been gone a week, and the funeral was just yesterday. She's processing the events and the impact this is going to have on her life."

"What about her belief that she saw him even though he'd already died? Or the fact that she talks to him, even though he's dead?"

Todd leaned forward. *Ooops.* He'd gotten Cassie in trouble again. That he hadn't intended to, didn't matter. Although, Dr. Sanchez surprised him. She seemed to understand. Maybe he could talk to Cassie, explain what the doctor had said. Dr. Sanchez might be able to help Cassie. Maybe even bring her closer to her mother.

He tuned in again to the conversation going on around him.

"That's normal. It's her way of coping as she accepts her new reality. As long as she's not suicidal, she needs to be given as much time and space as she needs." The doctor started to stand when Tom interrupted her.

"What about her obsession with finding out what happened to her friend? She doesn't believe the police. She's been asking questions, going to the sheriff's office and who knows what else?"

"Denial is also normal." Dr. Sanchez settled deeper into her chair. "If she believes she knows her friend better than the rest of you, and her knowledge doesn't fit with the image of what everyone else is saying, she has to find an explanation in order to move forward."

Abby reached a hand to Tom. "How do we handle this?"

Todd leaned forward. This was the test of Dr. Sanchez. If she got this right, then Todd would recommend Cassie go and see her for sure.

"Give her time." Dr. Sanchez smiled at the two blank faces. "Quit thinking of her as damaged or ill. She's fine. Yes, she could use my help, but more to speed up the process than anything. For what she's been through, she's doing amazingly well. What you don't want to do is alienate her any further. If you want a relationship with her again, you'll need to make sure there's a pathway that she's going to be willing to travel. Ease up on the discipline, the yelling at her. Don't stare at her all the time to see how she's doing. Be natural."

Cassie's father frowned, his gaze flitting between the doctor and his wife. Abby chewed her bottom lip and stared at the floor.

Todd grinned and clapped his hands slowly. She was good.

Perfect.

CHAPTER TEN

Cassie wandered aimlessly through the mall. She hadn't bothered to contact her friends. She didn't want to be with anyone except Todd. The only person in the whole world who'd understood her before and might understand what she was going through now was gone.

She couldn't even call him. Unless there was a dial-hell-on-earth number somewhere.

Her mind touched briefly on this morning's disaster before ruthlessly slamming that door shut. She so wasn't going there.

Cassie stopped at the window of a specialty bathing suit shop and stared at the bikini on a plastic mannequin. Beach season was in a month or so. A couple of weeks ago, she'd wondered if she'd be too chubby for a bikini, and this week she wondered if she'd lost so much weight that the bra might cave inward for a lack of anything to keep its shape. How sad was that? She'd been so proud when she'd finally started developing, years after Penny. And now she resembled a scrawny twelve-year-old again. Did people lose ten pounds in a week?

Maybe that's what had her mom worried.

Cassie surveyed her reflection and had to admit, her hair, although clean, hung limp to her shoulders. She should have put it up in a ponytail. Her eyes had the same black circles under them as yesterday. Yeah, that might give her mother cause for concern.

Groaning, Cassie rubbed her cheeks until they flushed pink. She really did have a scarecrow thing going on. The food court was only a couple of corners away. She needed food, since she hadn't finished her toast this morning. A muffin would go down nicely right now.

A few minutes later she found an empty table and took a small bite. Blueberry. Yum. She took a second taste of muffin, relishing that same explosion of flavor she'd experienced with her toast this morning.

"Well, well, well. Look who's here."

Three of Todd's druggy friends pulled up chairs and sat beside her. One pulled her plate away and the other snagged her coffee cup.

"Hey," she protested, snatching the muffin off the plate. "What are you doing?"

"Well, little Miss Snoopy here hasn't been listening. So we're paying you a second visit." Brodie sneered, his eyes dead cold.

Brodie terrified the crap out of her. He had a way of looking at her as if she were nothing. As if he'd just as soon step on her, like a bug. She'd asked Todd about him once. His explanation had more to do with having known each other since they were small children than anything to do with liking the guy. More like a routine that had developed into a bad habit over time. Only Todd wasn't here now to rein him in.

"Yeah, siccing the police on us wasn't very smart of you." Aric took a sip of her coffee while she watched. His face punched up like her neighbor's pug.

She laughed. "Not man enough to drink the real stuff, huh?"

The cup landed on the table with enough effort to splat coffee all over everything. She glared at them all. "What is your problem?"

Goth Dory snickered, her black makeup rippled like a clown. She leaned forward in a parody of meanness that came off as pathetic instead. "Don't you be going and telling the cops about us. They came to my door yesterday asking all kinds of questions."

"Then answer the stupid questions. The cops don't need to be told about you three. Crap, you're on the top of the teenage wanted list as far as they're concerned. You'll all be doing adult time before the year is out. I never did see what Todd saw in you guys. Drunk driving, theft, drugs." She sneered at them. "Maybe one of you left Todd to die on the side of that hill, while you ran off to save your lousy hides. Vehicular manslaughter, if you had anything to do with it. Great addition to your rap sheet. Kill your best friend and leave him to die alone." Cassie snorted, pissed as hell and grateful to have a direction to blow. She didn't know if there would be any charges for something like that, she sure as hell wished there would be.

"What the hell are you talking about?" Aric sputtered, sitting up indignantly. "We didn't have nothing to do with that."

"Yeah, like I'm going to believe a thief like you." Cassie snorted in disgust, her eye on the other two exchanging silent looks. "You're such a tool, Aric. Your friends are going to ruin your life and you don't even see it coming." Cassie stood up, dumped the rest of her muffin on the table in front of them, spreading the coffee puddle further. She bent down and shoved her face in Dory's. "I haven't spoken to the cops – yet. However stay the hell away from me or I will. Friends of Todd's or not. He didn't deserve to die like that. You don't scare me."

She stood up and strode off.

"She's fucking nuts, man. We had nothing to do with Todd's death."

"What's her deal anyway? She's totally flipped."

Their words followed her down the corridor.

Cassie hoped they'd had nothing to do with the accident. The truth was, they did scare her, but she wasn't about to let them threaten her. Losers.

***

Gerome Magnusson frowned. There was no evidence that Todd Spence had company in the vehicle at the time of the accident. There was circumstantial evidence Todd had been drinking at the time. Except if he had been drunk, could he have climbed out of the vehicle on his own? Drunks led charmed lives and the alcohol often blunted their pain. But as injured as he was? And if he'd made it that far, couldn't he have made it up the hill?

Opening the file in front of him, he searched for the coroner's report. No tox screens had come back yet. Todd had come in reeking. Everyone knew Todd; knew his father. The case was supposed to be simple. Open and shut. Todd had been literally doused in alcohol, his hair, his clothing, even inside his mouth. This wasn't just a simple case of a broken bottle, its contents spread everywhere.

He'd sustained multiple fractures. Several ribs, femur, dislocated shoulder and a skull fracture.

Gerome closed his eyes and tried to put himself in that vehicle with those injuries. Could he have gotten himself out? The leg had broken above the knee joint. The broken ribs would have been painful but they wouldn't have incapacitated him. Now the skull fracture was iffy. So was the collarbone – for climbing anyway. With only one of these injuries on its own it could be possible. Together though, that was a different story. Still, he'd seen some pretty big miracles happen when people fought for survival.

They'd assumed the boy had been thrown out during the somersaulting motion of the vehicle as it went down the hill. He sat back and considered that for a moment. If that had been the case, surely he'd have been thrown out somewhere along the path and not at the bottom where the vehicle had come to its final resting place. Not to mention the position in which he'd been found. Todd had been found on his back, arms and legs straight – as if laid out.

That's what was wrong. Would this kid have gotten into that position on his own? It would be the first time he'd heard of such a thing happening.

People *did* survive a hell of a lot – especially when panic drove them to superhuman efforts. Todd had been a healthy active young man and he'd been one of only two men to die on that corner.

He frowned. That's what that young girl had said. What was her name again? He clicked on her email, ignoring the eighteen others waiting for his attention. Cassie Merchant. Right. She'd suggested that Todd might not have been the driver, but she didn't have any explanation when she'd also said he never let anyone else drive his car. Yet the kids Todd was with on the last night said Todd had always been the designated driver. He frowned, remembering what another group of kids had said.

They'd made Todd seem like a split personality. Doing drugs and alcohol all the time. A high school bad boy who would not have graduated, no matter what he'd told everyone else.

That he could check out, unfortunately not until Monday. He'd attended the funeral, unsurprised by the small turnout. Todd hadn't been great friends with anyone except Cassie. He'd been friendly with many, only that wasn't the same thing.

The cell phone, if Todd had it sitting beside him in the vehicle or in a holder on the dash – and not in his pocket – would have burned to a crisp in the inferno. Although, there should have been some sign of it. The vehicle hadn't been moved until mid-morning on the next day. They didn't exactly have the same services that any big city would have. Besides, the case had looked to be straight forward.

He had to admit, though, only Cassie had stirred up a pile of doubts.

Her last email was a concern, though. She thought there was a potential witness to the accident, or at least very close after.

He knew Martha and Peter Cunningham pretty well. If they'd seen something important, they'd have come forward.

Cassie said they'd never heard back from Peter and she wanted to find out for sure. She planned on talking to Martha herself.

Martha was dying, and Peter wouldn't take kindly to anyone bothering her. They valued their privacy – and then some.

With a disgusted sigh, he reached for the phone. "I'd better nip this one in the bud before she goes and brings on more trouble."

***

Jessie hated this part. He'd decided to do this and he would, but, damn it, he didn't want to. Visiting his father was at the bottom of the things in life he enjoyed. Still if his mother didn't have Todd's cell phone and the deputy and the coroner's office didn't, then the only place left, *if* it was going to be found, was at his dad's house. Personally, he didn't see it surviving the crash-and-burn of the accident. That brought him to the other reason he didn't want to do this. It was a waste of time.

Cassie wouldn't lay off though. If there were a cell phone to find, she wanted to make sure it was found. She had a point. There'd be a record of any incoming and outgoing calls. The police could get that if they wanted to. Although there were considerations to be made about budgets and costs in doing something like that. Especially when the sheriff was likely to close this one quickly, given the people involved. Without Deputy Magnusson's involvement, the file would have been slammed shut already.

Finding the phone just made sense.

Jessie knocked on the front door of his dad's duplex, noting his old man's rusted-out pickup parked in the carport, full of cans and bags. What a pigsty. Still, this had been Todd's life not his. He frowned at that thought as he pounded on the door again. Had Todd liked his life or hated it? Had he wanted to live with Mom? Jessie knew he'd have hated living with his alcoholic-bum-of-a-father. And Todd had been a chip of the old block.

Or had he?

Was he as guilty as everyone else of believing that Todd could never be anything except a younger clone of his derelict parent? Did that imply Jessie would have the same problem? Was there no choice in life? He hated to think that he'd been letting his mother's fear-based opinions get to him.

She'd suddenly gone on this binge of believing Jessie needed his father in his life, needed a strong man to shake him in the opposite direction that his brother had gone. Illogical and stupid. As if having Dad around had helped Todd? Not. His mother hoped Dad would quit drinking so he could be there for Jessie.

He pounded the door again. This time it opened under the force of his fist. As usual, his father hadn't bothered to lock up. Jessie stuck his head inside. "Hello?" He peered around the door. "Dad, are you home?"

There was no answer. Jessie hated the hollowness, the cold atmosphere that lived here. Every time he came, the emptiness of the place creeped him out – even when his father was home. His father's soul was as empty as the bottles strewn around the house. It didn't matter where you looked, the bottom of a bottle stared back at you. His mom might be right, thinking that he could benefit from having a father around. She was wrong in thinking this one was the right one.

Jessie walked through the kitchen and into the living room. He stopped at the archway and stared. The house couldn't be called clean the last few times he'd been here, although there'd often been evidence that someone had tried to tame the chaos. No such attempt had been made recently. Newspapers, clothing and remnants of old food decorated the place – with empty bottles as permanent fixtures. And boy was it heavily decorated.

Taking a couple of more steps inside the room, stepping around pizza boxes and Chinese takeout cartons, Jessie peered into the gloomy interior. A heavy snuffle startled him. He peered over the back of the couch. His father was sleeping off his latest drunk – if the size of the bottle cemetery heaped at his side was any indication.

A soundless whistle escaped at the sheer volume of alcohol consumed. This man could do some serious drinking. Jessie tried to search the living room for the phone, only there was too much stuff to move. He gave a cursory look through the kitchen before going upstairs to his brother's room. How long had it been since he'd been in here last? At least a year. Maybe two or three even.

This had to be the cleanest room in the house. Jessie slouched against the doorjamb and surveyed the area. A single bed, computer, dresser and night table. Not a whole lot of personality with its bare walls in plain white and no curtain covering the window. A window that stood wide open. Though fresh air was nice, this was beyond that. Had his dad been in here since Todd's death?

It hurt to look at his brother's room. So at odds with the rest of the house and with the impression his brother gave out. A front? Was this cold empty room more indicative of who his brother really was? Lonely. Needing to be in control and careful with his things. That fit with Cassie's comments. Maybe, she *had* known his brother better than anyone. Especially him.

Not wanting to be in the house when his father woke up, Jessie quickly opened a few dresser drawers and searched the night table. Nothing. Not that he'd expected anything. Todd, like every other teenager Jessie knew, used to have the cell phone implanted somewhere on his body. Jessie had the same problem. He checked his cell phone every few minutes like every other teen he knew.

Cassie was right again. That cell phone would have been on Todd. Not loose on the seat beside him. Not in a holder on the dash. That wasn't Todd's style. It would have been in Todd's pocket. Todd's pants pocket. No teenager would keep his cell phone in a shirt pocket. A jacket pocket maybe, a hoodie pocket for sure, but not a shirt pocket.

Todd had to have had it on him when he was killed. If it hadn't burned in the crash, been lost at the accident site, turned up at the morgue, been placed with his personal belongings, or to be found at his house – and sure, he'd have to ask his dad when he sobered up – the only other option he could think of was that someone had taken it.

Whoever did it had to have been there at the time of Todd's death – or right after. That meant someone who'd seen the accident or had been walking along the highway or – and this was starting to look more likely – had been in the car with his brother.

However, just because someone may have picked up Todd's phone didn't mean they'd had anything to do with the accident. There could have been a passerby who'd helped Todd out of the vehicle, then tried to use his cell phone to call in the accident. Had Todd's wallet been on him? Money?

Jessie frowned as he stared around his brother's sparsely finished bedroom. If someone had emptied his pockets, would the cops know? Would they have even looked? Todd had been through a horrible accident. Who'd have even considered if something had been stolen? Everything else had burned. No evidence. No proof.

If he'd seen an accident, what would he do? Go down and see if he could help. Call the cops, and if he didn't have a phone, check to see if the injured guy did. Make the call...and then what? Would he really have tried to wrestle the phone back into the prone man's pocket? Not likely. More likely, he'd have tossed it on the ground beside the man or hung onto it, thinking to pass it on later.

Maybe the police had traced the phone number and seen if it had been used since. He smacked his head with his hand. Why didn't he just call the damn phone and see if someone answered. Cassie said she'd done that many times already.

Had she lately?

He pulled out his cell phone, only to realize he didn't have his brother's number. Still he had Cassie's. Quickly he texted her, asking her to call his brother's phone so he could see if it was at his dad's house. After a minute he put his phone on vibrate and texted, asking her to confirm when she'd done it. His phone vibrated before he could send the text. "Cassie?"

"Yes. I'll call Todd's number now. Stay there and listen for the ring – it's a Star Wars theme."

His phone went dead. Jessie looked at the silent grave-of-a-room for several minutes and then headed out of the house. He didn't want to wake his father. At the kitchen, he stopped and waited only there was still no ringing phone. It wasn't here.

With his phone still on vibrate, he waited until Cassie called him, then exited out the back door before answering. "Cassie, what did you find out?"

Cassie's excitement raced through the phone. "A woman answered. She said I had a wrong number and hung up. But at least we know his phone is out there. Someone has it." She was almost shrieking at the end.

Jessie held the phone slightly away from his ear, grinning. "That's great news. Did you happen to recognize her voice?"

More subdued, Cassie responded, "No. Honestly, she sounded kind of old, crotchety, you know."

Old. That threw him. "Maybe Todd lost it before the accident. Is that possible?"

Cassie considered the question, then said, "I can ask his friends, those he was with that night. He'd have had his phone then."

"Do you have their numbers?"

"Some, but I'll ask them in person, at school tomorrow."

"At least we know it didn't burn up in the fire. Cassie, did Todd carry a lot of money around on him?"

"What do you mean by a lot? He didn't blow wads of money, but he always had some cash."

"I just wondered if someone went down to the accident, saw Todd lying there and checked him over, maybe even went through his wallet and snatched his cell phone…"

"Ughh. That's a horrible thought."

"It could be innocent. Maybe they used his cell phone to call for help. My mom has his wallet and I remember her looking at it and saying 'typical.' When I asked her what she meant, she said that she never let me run around without at least a twenty in my pocket."

"Todd usually had cash for coffee or lunch."

"Hmmm. It might be nothing, but if you're talking to his friends, find out if they'd ordered pizza or something. Todd might have picked up the tab. The phone and money thing are just bugging me." Jessie looked up. He had to cross the road, walk a couple more blocks then he'd be home. "Let's talk tomorrow, Cassie. I've got to go."

CHAPTER ELEVEN

Cassie didn't sleep well. An uneasy truce was in effect between her and her parents. They acted as if nothing had happened. Totally weird.

Early Monday, Penny texted, asking to twin their clothing. Cassie agreed, hoping it would put her in a better mood. They'd chosen blue and black, so Cassie took pains with her appearance and pulled her hair up into a high ponytail. Penny would do the same.

She was running late, so skipped breakfast, grabbed a granola bar and raced out of the house. Penny met her half way to school.

The two girls grinned at each other. "Perfect way to start a boring day."

"True. So how come you wouldn't go out with us on Saturday?"

Cassie rolled her eyes and explained about her parents having sprung the shrink on her.

"They didn't? Without talking to you first?" Penny was horrified. "How could they do that?"

"The element of surprise." The two girls shook their heads, groaning at the stupidity of parents. At the school gates, Goth Dory waited for Cassie.

"Penny, go on ahead," Dory said.

"Hell no. If you've got something to say to Cassie you can say it in front of me, too." Penny glared at the gangly girl, who was wearing her usual black from head to toe.

Dory stuck her chin out to stare Penny down before glancing over at Cassie. "I have something to say about Todd, but I won't speak if she's here."

Taking her measure, Cassie said to Penny. "Please. Just go up and wait on the stairs for me. I won't be long."

Penny opened her mouth, took a good look at Cassie's face then turned and brushed past them. Several steps past, she slowed uncertainly and twisted to look back, with a questioning expression on her face. Cassie gave her tiny smile, an encouraging nod. Penny frowned, tilted her head toward Dory and mouthed, *"Be careful."*

With a quick grin, Cassie turned to Dory. "What's up?"

"We didn't have anything to do with Todd's death. We wouldn't have." Dory's faced twisted. "He was our friend, too."

"So why the threats? Why act as if you have something to hide?" Cassie asked reasonably.

"We don't want the cops asking questions. That's all. It's got nothing to do with Todd or his death." She searched the surrounding area, as if afraid of being seen. She turned back to Cassie, "Why are you asking all these questions, anyway?"

"Because I know Todd didn't drink and drive. You may have been his friend, however, you obviously didn't know him well enough if you believe that garbage. How many times did he come and give rides to you and the others because you'd been drinking?"

At Dory's dawning understanding, Cassie pursed her lips, giving a decisive nod. "That's right. He wasn't alone when he died. Someone was there and someone knows something. Until they speak, I'll keep pushing."

"That's a good way to get yourself in trouble," Dory warned. "If someone was with him, they aren't going to appreciate you meddling. Depending on their role in this, they might be facing major jail time."

"As long as it wasn't you or your friends." She leveled a serious glance at Dory, "But if it was you, then trouble is coming your way."

Dory glanced around nervously. "We saw Todd that night."

"What?" Cassie asked. She leaned closer, hissing, "When?"

"After he dropped Ivan off at home. He was just pulling away from the curb when we crossed the road to talk to him. We talked for a few minutes. That's all. We talked."

"Did he give you a ride somewhere?"

"No, not at all. Aric talked with him for a bit, then he drove off."

"Did you happen to see if he had his cell phone?" Cassie waited anxiously for the answer.

"A call came in as we spoke. He looked at the caller ID, frowned, said he had to go and took off talking on the phone."

"Any idea who called him? Did you hear any of the conversation?" Excitement twisted her whisper into a small shriek. She looked around to see if they attracted any attention.

"No, I didn't. All I can say is he looked pissed off." Dory took several steps back. "I've got to go to class. Leave us alone. I've told you everything I know."

"Make you sure you tell your buddies to leave me alone, too. I'm not trying to bring any trouble to your door, but if it takes me there, I won't hold back. Todd was too important to me."

"Yeah, I get it." Dory loped ahead to race past Penny and through the front doors of the school.

Cassie followed at a more sedate pace. They'd been right. Todd's night had been more exciting than it had first seemed.

She joined Penny and together they entered the school.

She needed to contact Jessie. First she would check with Todd's other friends.

Someone knew something.

***

Todd watched Cassie rush through her school day, so distracted she almost goofed on a Chemistry test she hadn't even known was scheduled for today. At the last minute of the test, when she realized she'd made a mistake, her eyes widened in horror. She erased in a panic, before scribbling the correct equations down.

He hoped she'd gotten it right that time. Cassie was a great student. Not a geeky one, a realistic one. She made low nineties, with the occasional wild perfect score thrown in. Rarely did she find herself at the very top of the class. Always in the top three or four though. She had a future lined up for herself. A vet, he thought. She'd be so good at that. Although, he worried about the high suicide rate amongst veterinarians. Or was that with dentists?

Why would anyone willingly quit such a great experience? Now that he sat on the other side, the side of no return, Todd wished there was a way to show all these people how mistaken they were in taking their own lives. Life was worth so much. A value that couldn't be appreciated until it was lost.

Like he hadn't valued his.

If he could do it all over again, he'd find time to enjoy more. Not just friends like Cassie, but the most simple things; like the morning after a fresh rain, puttering around on his car, honoring those dreams he never put time into. He'd always wanted a dog, had hoped to try parachuting; he'd planned on taking a coast to coast trip – all things he'd never have a chance to experience now.

And his world was changing. Now it had a muted effect, like cotton stuffed in his ears. That made it difficult to hear conversations even when he was standing right beside the people.

Like with Cassie and Dory this morning. He'd heard that conversation, barely. Then there was all the stuff everyone wasn't saying. He didn't have the same intuitive senses anymore or the same ability to catch subtle body language and innuendos, as if he were less now than he had been when alive.

He tried to concentrate. Dory had said they'd spoken to him. A flash of laughter and joking while he was sitting in the car slipped into his thoughts. She was right. He'd spoken to them on the streets a few houses away from Ivan's place.

He dragged through his memories, searching for the topic of conversation. He pulled up fragments of a conversation about a party they invited him to. He'd refused but they'd asked him to reconsider.

Todd paused. Had he changed his mind? That might explain the drinking but *not* the driving. Nor, as he gave it more thought, did it explain the time frame. According to what he understood, he'd crashed between 11:15 and 11:30 pm. He'd dropped Ivan off about a half hour earlier. Not enough time to go to the party and leave and still reach that dangerous corner of the road at the right time. Or to have drunk much.

Dory and friends might have eaten up five minutes. He had no idea about the rest. Dory had mentioned a phone call? Who'd have called him at that hour?

He struggled to remember. In his mind, he could hear his phone and see himself pulling it out of his pocket and talking, only he couldn't see the number in his mind. Or remember any feelings attached to the event. A girl, maybe? That wasn't unheard of when one of his 'friends' wanted to play on a Friday night. Todd couldn't remember a time he'd said 'no.' But Dory said he'd been pissed, so it wouldn't likely have been a female as he was always very amiable anticipating those sessions, knowing he'd get lucky if he played his cards right.

Who could have pissed him off? Todd hopped up onto the window ledge in the Chemistry lab as the as the kids streamed out of class around and through him. He stuck his legs straight out. Two guys walked through his knees and never noticed. Todd checked the various looks on the kids' faces. He saw everything from relief that the test was over to anger that the test had happened in the first place.

Kids at his age notoriously felt injured in one way or another. It didn't take much to set them off. Learning that adults controlled almost everything made them irritable, frustrated and most of all – pissed.

Who'd have pissed him off?

Like the rest of these kids, the answer was anyone and anything, on any given day.

***

Cassie searched the common areas for Ivan, Bryce and Rob. She finally ran them down at the far back corner. Of course.

"Hey? How are you guys doing?"

Bryce shrugged. "It's a little easier. Still reach for the phone to text him sometimes before I remember."

"Yeah, me, too. And sometimes I think he's sitting there watching us. It's kinda cool, yet at the same time it's really freaky." Rob gave a mock shudder.

Cassie stared at Rob, amazement on her face.

"What?" he said, defensively. "I'm not losing it. He was my friend and sometimes I feel like he's still there for me."

She smiled, a huge sense of relief in her heart. Todd *was* missed; he'd *had* good friends. He'd be delighted to know that. In fact, he obviously did know if Rob was sensing his presence. That meant Todd had been visiting them, too. Why couldn't they see him? Or did they see him, then toss him off as a figment of their imagination?

Or perhaps Todd did not appear to them at all.

Sighing, Cassie plunked down heavily beside the guys on the foamy couch. "It's hard. I find myself talking to him when he's not there."

"Yeah."

"What did you guys do that last night? Just hang out and play games, eat pizza and hassle each other?" She tried to make it sound like casual interest. People strode past, some moved between the group, all walked toward their own friends.

"Yeah. We'd been gaming for hours. We were just talking about ordering in pizza when my dad said to pack it in." Rob spoke up, slouching to the point he was almost falling off the chair. The other two who nodded their heads, slumped just as ridiculously.

"Yeah, Todd had even offered to pay for it. He always pitched in. This time he said it was his treat." Ivan reached over and kicked Rob lightly.

He grinned. "I enjoyed that. We'd been hassling each other since forever about making Todd pay because he had more money than any of us."

Cassie straightened up. "I thought he had to go to the bank."

"Yeah, we walked there after school. He had a paycheck to put in." Ivan looked over at Bryce. "Did your boss ever hire anyone to replace Todd?"

"Not yet. Get your application in and I'll give you a good reference with him."

"Kinda feels weird, dude. Like I don't want to take his job." Ivan slumped lower, flicking his cell phone around in his hand.

"Todd hated that job. He'd laugh his head off and say go for it, if he knew." Cassie laughed.

"Yeah, do it." Bryce urged. "She's right. Todd would think it was great."

"Maybe. I'll think about it."

Cassie sat and visited a little longer.

At least she knew Todd had money when he'd left their place. So, where was it now?

***

Jessie found himself unable to keep his attention on classes or friends today. Damn Cassie, anyway. That smile of hers pulled at him; her personality intrigued him; her loyalty to his brother had brought her very close to his heart.

That was a dangerous place. He didn't want her to see him just as Todd's brother. On the other hand, he highly suspected he'd take Cassie any way he could have her.

His mom had mentioned Cassie a time or two. Saying what a lovely girl she appeared to be and, Jessie had loved this part...she wondered how had Todd hooked up with such a nice girl? It had given him pause when he saw the evidence to support her view of Todd.

Sad.

His cell phone rang. Cassie? He dug out his phone and groaned. Greeaat; it was his boss. They needed him to come into the store a half hour early to relieve Joe, who needed to go home early. Agreeing, he closed his phone as a text came in. Cassie.

Jessie grinned and went to read it when his phone was snatched out of his hand.

"Dude, who the hell is putting that look on your face?" Stephen looked at the text, puzzled, before comprehension hit. "Jessie, are you nuts? This is...was your brother's girl."

"I know that. We're just friends." Pissed, Jessie snatched it back and read the message. Something about having talked with Dory and friends already and that she was having no luck in finding the others yet. She was on the hunt now.

"So what's going on here?"

Jessie frowned. "What? We're just friends?"

Stephen shook his head, making his long hair fly around. "Ah, no."

Jessie gave him a disgusted look. "It's not like that. She wants to talk about Todd. That's all."

"You *said* your brother was just a loser asshole."

Faced with his own prejudices, Jessie swallowed hard. "I know what I said – now that he's gone, well, I'm forced to re-evaluate."

Stephen punched him lightly on his shoulder. "That sounds deep. I can see you might have a few regrets."

"Yeah. There are a few of those. Cassie's okay."

"Long as you remember she's been his."

"Not the way you mean it."

"Dude, they were friends for years. Todd had 'em all."

"Not Cassie." Jessie didn't know how or why, but he knew they hadn't been lovers. Todd had cared about Cassie. Too much to make her one of his short-term playthings. He had other girls for that. No, Cassie had been special to him.

And she was becoming special for Jessie, too.

CHAPTER TWELVE

Cassie?"

Cassie turned around to see Todd slightly behind her. "Hey." Searching the area, she checked to make sure no one was in hearing distance. For the same reason, she turned down the alleyway that led to their special park. Surely she'd be able to talk to him there without being seen.

"How are you doing? And did you try to talk to the other people on your side?" Although how there could be sides when he stood right in front of her, she didn't know.

"I tried to, only I can't seem to communicate. They can see me, they react with a smile or frown, but they don't open their mouths and talk. It's like they already know their limitations. When I asked several questions they never answered. So I gave up."

Turning her head, Cassie winced at his oozing frustration. "Keep trying. Maybe they're communicating in another way, telepathically? Maybe they're waiting for you to learn how?"

He slid her a sideways look. "So, it's all about me now?" His grin flashed. "Just kidding. You could be right." He tilted his head. "Although, it's been just over a week, I'm not seeing the same people anymore. Maybe we only get a certain amount of time here. To work through our transition, say our good-byes. That sort of thing."

Cassie's heart ached. This was going to end sometime, she knew that. But she didn't want it to. How selfish.

"Speaking of which, I stayed to listen to the conversation between your parents and Dr. Sanchez on Saturday."

"Oh great. Just what I wanted to know," she muttered under her breath.

"I heard that. How come I can hear you so much better than everyone else? Besides, you *should* want to hear about this." He related the conversation he'd heard, finishing with, "So I think you should go and see her. At least talk to her once or twice and see how you feel. If she can make this easier on you, why not, right?"

She slowed her steps. He'd given her something to ponder. That didn't mean she was ready to jump in and see this woman. Although, it made her feel better to hear her parents were given such good advice. Since the doctor was an adult, it made sense that she could speak 'adult' better than 'teenager.'

"I'm not saying you have to continue seeing her. Maybe just give her a chance. I'm not sure how much longer I'm going to be able to hang around, and I'd feel better to know you have someone to help you get over this."

"I don't want to talk about you not being here," she snapped, shoving her fists deep into the pockets of her hoodie.

"Of course you don't." His voice managed to come across both dry and humorous.

"Sorry." She held herself tight for a long moment and took a deep breath before releasing it slowly. "It's just hard to contemplate."

"Which is why I think you should go and just see her. Sit there in silence, if you want, and see how you feel being in her space. If she says anything to you the wrong way, get up and walk out. No one's forcing you. I'd just feel better if you considered it."

She studied his serious expression. The old Todd would never have suggested something like this. This new Todd seemed older and maybe, if she admitted it to herself, wiser. Would it hurt her to go and talk with this woman?

She had to be in control of this. She didn't want to say anything about seeing Todd in his ghostly form. This woman might be a shrink and had probably heard it all by now, only this was private. Personal. And maybe she was losing it and Todd wasn't really walking beside her with that concerned I-want-only-what's-best-for-you look on his face.

"Okay, I'll consider it."

"Good. That's all I ask. I think it would be best for you to actually talk to this woman, but..." he moved back a step at her glare, "I'm not pushing it."

"Right." Cassie sped up as she saw the old swing set come into view. She couldn't resist racing toward it. "Last one's a rotten egg." She arrived at the swings breathless and laughing to find Todd already sitting and waiting, a big grin on his face.

Her heart warmed. She said, "You cheated?"

"Did not."

"Did too."

"How could I? I don't even exist in your world anymore. Is it my fault I don't have slow heavy legs to lug my oversized body around? No. I can move faster than you because I'm not restricted like you are. That doesn't mean I cheated," he said loftily.

Cassie laughed. "How typical. Twist everything around to suit yourself. Can you think about a place and then just find you're there?"

"Yeah, something like that."

"Sweet. I could use that trick getting to and from school or heading to the mall."

"Yeah, except that, because of the way you'd get that skill, you'd no longer have a reason to go to the mall or anywhere else, for that matter." His sober face stared at her. "Remember, you'd be dead – like me."

***

Adam Spence stared at his face in the mirror. His son was dead. His ex-wife was a nagging bitch. His youngest son was a thief. He'd come into Adam's own home and left again when Adam hadn't been there. Or, his conscious reminded him, when he'd been asleep. What was he to do with that information?

He wouldn't have known except Todd's bedroom door was open, his drawers were left askew and he'd found a piece of paper that had obviously fallen out of Jessie's pocket onto the floor. Though he might not have spent much time with his youngest in the last few years, he sure as hell knew his writing. His mom made him write letters and cards incessantly. Adam would have preferred in-person-visits and Jessie, he was sure, would have preferred to send an impersonal email.

So neither of them got what they wanted.

Why had Jessie come here? What had he been after? And more to the point, what had he taken?

***

Deputy Magnusson hung up the phone and tried to clean up his hurried notes. He couldn't explain to himself why he was still pursuing Cassie's faint hope, but by now, lodged somewhere in his brain was an acceptance that her theory was quite possible, and maybe they'd done this kid a wrong.

The sheriff didn't agree. He hated Adam Spence something fierce and refused to consider that the son wasn't exactly the same as the father. Before storming out this morning, he'd made his opinion damn clear.

"Damn nuisance, these kids," he'd said. "Think they can do whatever they want without paying the consequences. Well, this little bastard got what was coming to him. I'm not wasting any taxpayer money on the damn case. He was alone and covered in alcohol and he crashed. Simple. Put it down as an accident, if that makes you feel better, but that damn kid had been drinking."

Gerome could still hear the rattling of the walls when he thought about those words.

Only Gerome didn't have the same prejudice. And he didn't think much of not doing a proper job of things. More than that, someone might be getting away with something they shouldn't be.

He added the new sheet to Todd's file, and made a notation in his notebook to bring it up with the sheriff. The investigator said the airbags had deployed and deflated properly.

There'd been blood on the airbag. There'd been blood everywhere. As much as he wanted to get it tested for DNA, the county's budget didn't extend to supporting suppositions like this one. This wasn't a murder. This was an accident brought on by the victim himself. Supposedly.

Cassie had filled him on Todd's cell phone, explaining that one call she made was answered by an older woman, proving the cell phone hadn't been destroyed in the fire. So how had the woman gotten hold of it?

He turned the information over and over in his head, searching out and destroying different scenarios. It still came back to who answered Todd Spence's cell, and how had the cell phone come into their possession? And did any of it matter? Todd was still dead.

***

Todd sat in the deputy's spare chair and wondered how to tell him to keep looking. How to tell the deputy to believe in him. To believe that Todd hadn't been drinking and driving. The deputy appeared to be honest. He was Maggie's dad. Maggie was pretty cool, even though her dad was in law enforcement.

How did Maggie communicate with someone like that? Not that Todd could use the same methods. He tried to move a piece of paper that sat on the deputy's file. It wouldn't budge. He tried to blow on the paper. Nothing.

"Hello? Can you hear me?"

The deputy groaned.

Todd leaned forward in amazement. "Hello? Hello?"

The deputy shut the file and leaned back on his chair. "Drinking and driving huh? Stupid."

"What's stupid?"

"The sheriff's not happy. To ask for more man-hours to keep looking would just piss him off more. *The case is closed, Gerome.*"

His mimic made Todd grin. He liked this guy. Now if only he'd keep working on Todd's case.

CHAPTER THIRTEEN

Cassie walked in the direction of the main street. Living in a small town meant not a lot went on, and there weren't many things to do or see – particularly after school, like now. On the other hand, it made it easier to go to places without her parents.

The only way she'd stop in and talk to this doctor was if no one was around. And that meant no one, including Todd. If he wanted her to check out this woman, then he wasn't allowed to listen in either.

The small door of the brick brownstone was surprisingly cozy looking, instead of intimidating and clinical as she'd expected. Cassie hesitated briefly. Opening the door, she stepped inside. She hoped the doctor was still there and available, although the sign on the door said the clinic would be closing any minute.

The waiting room had the appearance of a living room, not an office. Couches, coffee tables – even a television. Not a wealthy, cold interior or a sparsely furnished room like she'd expected. The front reception was empty. She leaned over, searching for a bell. There didn't appear to be one.

"Hello?"

She frowned, waited a long moment, not sure what to do. Could everyone have left for the day and forgotten to lock the door?

"Cassie. How nice to see you." Dr. Sanchez strolled into the reception room, a gentle smile on her face.

Glancing at the door behind her, Cassie wished she'd bolted when she had the chance. She didn't know what to say.

"Uh, thanks. I'm not exactly sure why I'm here, to be honest."

Dr. Sanchez walked to the office chair and sat down, smiling up at her.

"Well, I'm glad you came." She busied herself pulling out a schedule and searching for a pencil. "Did you want to talk today or make an appointment for another time?"

With a light groan, Cassie said, "It needs to be now or I may talk myself out of returning."

That startled a laugh out of Dr. Sanchez. Offering Cassie an understanding smile, she said, "By all means, let's talk now."

"Uhm?" Cassie hated this next question. "Do I have to pay you or something? I don't know how this works." Shoving her hands in her pocket, she stood uncertainly in place.

Laughing lightly, Dr. Sanchez stood, motioning to a side door. "Don't worry about that. I've set it up with your parents already. Come on through to my office."

Cassie halted. She looked around the small cozy-looking room. "Would you mind if we talked here instead?"

Dr. Sanchez raised one eyebrow... Cassie didn't think much surprised her anymore.

"Sure." Dr. Sanchez walked out to the reception room and waved her hand wide. "Pick a seat."

Cassie chose the armchair in the corner. She knew there'd be some kind of psychological reasoning behind her choice and Dr. Sanchez would have taken note of it. Still, she'd come this far, she might as well go on.

"How are you doing at school?"

That wasn't what she wanted to talk about, however any opening worked. "School's okay. While it's difficult sometimes, in many ways it's no different from before."

"Does that bother you? That it's no different now?"

"Well, my world has changed so much, why hasn't everyone else's?" Her words, laced with resentment, surprised Cassie. She hadn't realized she'd been holding them in.

"I can see how that might be difficult."

"That's not the real issue. Everyone thinks Todd got what he deserved. Many say good riddance and make comments about how they're happy he's not here anymore."

The doctor had been writing notes. At Cassie's words, she raised her head and studied Cassie's face. "That would be hard for anyone. I wouldn't like to hear things like that about my friends, either."

"And some of those people *were* his friends. Then Todd had levels of friends."

"Explain what you mean by that, please."

Cassie settled deeper into her chair. "Todd had friends to party with. Friends to play games with. Friends to hang around at school with. And then there was me, his best friend."

"Did you have a problem with those other friends? Did you want to be one of them?" The doctor opened the small notebook Cassie hadn't even noticed she carried.

Cassie grinned. "Oh no. You see, I was the one that mattered all the time. The others only mattered some of the time. Todd and I could talk. About anything, anytime."

"And you don't have the same relationship with anyone else now, correct?"

"Correct." Cassie stared down at her hands folded in her lap like a young schoolgirl. "Before Todd, I had Grams."

"Ahh." Dr. Sanchez pulled a pen out of her pocket and wrote down a couple of things. "Death has taken a lot from you."

"Everything," Cassie cried out softly. "Everyone I cared about has died."

"What about your mother?"

"No."

"No?" Dr. Sanchez shifted backwards slightly. "What does that mean, Cassie?"

A slight frown whispered across Cassie's face despite her best attempts to not let it. She didn't like discussing her mother. She didn't do it willing with her friends and found it more uncomfortable with this doctor.

Grabbing her courage, Cassie opened up the one corner of her life she'd worked hard to forget. "My mother cares about my father and herself. Only. There is no room in their relationship for me. Any more than there was room for Grams."

"You don't feel loved?" The good doctor tilted her head, frowning.

"Yes, they love me. As much as they are capable. The problem, I guess, is that I'm needy. I need more. Grams was the same as me in that she also needed more than my parents could give. When I lost Grams, I effectively lost everything." A harsh laugh escaped. "Sorry, I don't mean to be dramatic. It's just when Grams died, it was obvious my mother didn't care. I couldn't stand to be close to her anymore."

"And does that bother you?"

Cassie tilted her head back to stare up at the ceiling. "I guess it must."

"Are your friends close to their moms?"

"Penny is super close. Her mom's the best. They can talk about anything. They have spa days, and shopping parties. Penny's dad is pretty cool, too. Cool in that he doesn't feel left out — or doesn't seem to," she added as an afterthought.

Dr. Sanchez grinned. "I'll have to remember that for when my daughter is older."

"Yeah, she'd probably enjoy that."

"So Penny gets to do special things with her mom and you don't do anything with yours?"

"Right."

"Hardly seems fair, does it?"

"My father would say something along the line of 'who said life was supposed to be fair?'" Cassie grinned at the sour look on Dr. Sanchez's face. "Something I'm sure you've heard before."

Dr. Sanchez smiled wryly. "Oh yes. Both my parents still like to remind me of that." Dr. Sanchez wrote down a few more things.

Watching her, Cassie wondered what could be so important.

"Have you ever spoken to your mother about how you feel?"

Cassie choked. "No. I find it hard to talk to her at all."

"Is that how you want the relationship to continue?"

Moving her feet up and down in front of her, Cassie stared at them moodily. "I don't know. If I could have a relationship like Penny has with her mom, maybe I'd change it. But it's too late now." Her breath puffed out of her mouth in a small burst. "So yeah, it might as well continue the way it is."

"And if it does, with Grams and Todd gone, you're going to be lonely. Lonely in a way you'll find quite difficult."

Pursing her lips, Cassie nodded. "True, but no matter what, my mother isn't going to replace Todd or my grandmother, so what choice do I have? Relationships like this are not formed overnight. I might turn more to Penny, or her mom even."

"Won't that cause trouble between Penny and you?"

She hadn't thought of that. "Possibly. I don't know. I'll have to see. Todd isn't replaceable, any more than Grams was."

A warm smile crossed the doctor's face. She pondered a moment, looking at Cassie, then put down her pencil and tilted her fingers under her chin.

"Why did you come here today?"

What to say? Cassie blinked several times, thinking. "I knew this scenario wouldn't end after walking out Saturday, and…"

"And," the doctor prompted.

Cassie sighed heavily. "It's what Grams and Todd would have wanted."

"Ahh." With one eyebrow raised, Dr. Sanchez, in a soft, so gentle voice, asked a much harder question, "Yes, but what does Cassie want?"

***

Jessie wandered throughout the house, lost.

"Are you alright, Jessie?" His mom had come up behind him, placing a hand on his shoulder. "Are you hungry?"

He groaned, throwing his hands up in the air. "No, Mom. Food won't fix everything."

"I know that. I'm sorry." She lifted her hand as if to touch him.

He stepped back. "I'm fine."

"No. You're not. I don't know what's wrong, but I'd like to." She chewed on her bottom lip. "Honey, I know this has been tough. I might be able to help, if you'd let me."

"I don't think there's anything anyone can do."

"Please don't say that." Her hand clenched on her blouse, and barely held her tears back. She looked for the world like a beaten puppy.

Jessie sighed. He didn't want to bring this up. Only he couldn't stand not knowing any longer. "Mom, why didn't you have anything to do with Todd?"

Her eyebrows raised in surprise. She sniffled once. "Well, I did. At least I tried to, but I'd left it too long. He was too hurt and didn't want anything to do with me."

"Why would you split us up the way you did? One child – one parent?"

His mother crossed her arms over her chest, gazing blindly out the window. "At the time, it seemed to be the best way to handle things. I was closer to you and Todd had become a handful. I thought he needed a stronger hand than I could give."

That made sense. Kind of. "Why not just move both of us back and forth between the two homes like everyone else did?"

"There was supposed to more interaction. Sundays together, Mom days and Dad days, only the divorce was so bitter. The arguing so bad, those special times days didn't happen."

"Ya think?"

"I'm sorry for my part in not keeping us together. At the time I was hurting, too. It was easier to leave everything alone. By the time I realized how distant everyone had become, it was too late to change."

Jessie listened, trying to understand, knowing that there was no way he could do what they'd done. He'd want to love both sons equally. Wouldn't everyone? Instead, when Todd had become a problem, along with Dad's increased drinking and violent behavior, his mom had been so relieved to put some distance between them, she'd smothered the child she had left and abandoned the other.

She'd been scared, misguided and wrong.

And his father's excuse? Who knew? It's not like anyone could talk to him anymore. He was committing suicide the hard way. "Was he always a drunk?"

"No," she whispered. "Not like this. Not until after the divorce." She turned to face him. "That was another reason to avoid working to keep the family close. He'd started drinking heavily. We couldn't count on him being sober when we visited or what he'd say while we were there."

"And yet you left Todd with him?"

"By that time Todd hated me and it was already too late. He refused to move back and I couldn't get your dad to quit drinking." She sniffled slightly. "I should have tried harder to get closer to him. But I didn't and now it's too late."

Jessie sighed. "I'm sorry. I didn't mean to bring back all those bad memories."

A hiccup of a laugh sounded. "Since Todd's death, I've thought of nothing else. Hated myself for letting him go. For not trying harder to be a family. Wondering what I could have done differently?" Another laugh escaped, a broken sound of a woman on the edge.

Jessie looked closely at his mom. She'd aged this last week, become fragile. He sensed she was close to a breakdown. He slid an arm around her thin shoulders and tugged her into his arms for a hug. He rested his head on the crown of her head.

"I'm sorry, Mom. I didn't mean to hurt you by bringing up painful topics."

"No, my dear Jessie. You didn't hurt me. I've hurt myself. And your father and Todd. For that I'm very sorry."

"Shhh." Jessie hugged her close. "It's going to be okay."

To his dismay, his mom burst into tears. Giving her slight frame a gentle squeeze, he let her cry for a moment, patting her back. "It's okay, Mom. Please stop."

She pulled away slightly, tears still running down her cheeks. She sniffled several times. "Oh Jessie, how can you say it's going to be okay. Todd is dead. It won't ever be okay again."

"I'm sorry," he said helplessly. "I'm not trying to make light of this, only to tell you it's not your fault."

"I wish I could believe that." She sniffled again, wiping her eyes on her sleeve.

Jessie reverted to a technique he'd learned years ago to distract his mother. "Mom, I don't suppose there's anything to eat in the house, is there?"

"What? Oh, are you hungry?" The tears dried up as she looked at him hopefully. "Of course there's something to eat. Let me go see what I can rustle up." With a warming smile, she wiped at her eyes again, and hurried across the room, her back straight and shoulders strong. A changed woman.

Jessie grinned. "A cup of tea would be good, too. Maybe a piece of cake or cookie for dessert?"

She stopped at the doorway and pivoted, brightness lighting up her face. "Oh yes. What a good idea. Give me a few minutes and I'll have something ready." She bustled off, happy.

For her, he would eat whatever she prepared, knowing that preparing the meal for him, helped her.

Now what was the best thing for him? He considered what Cassie was trying to do and why. He had as many reasons, if not more, to find out the truth. Not only had his family lost Todd, but his mother had allowed guilt over what she believed Todd had become to consume her. Even his dad no longer knew what bottle he drank from or why.

He needed to find the answers to the cause of Todd's death for his family's sake. Maybe then, after some time, they could heal and start again.

***

Cassie whipped through her Facebook stuff, laughing at several of her friends' comments. With the funeral over, the weekend recuperating, followed by the talk with Dr. Sanchez, Cassie actually felt like a heavy weight had fallen off her shoulders. She didn't know what had been the magical cure or if time had been the catalyst, yet she felt more at peace with Todd's death.

Not so much at the concept of him being something like the living dead though. She wanted to believe in reincarnation or heaven or some other happy answer, only it wasn't working out that way.

She'd spent her lunch hour in the school library trying to research life after death. She'd found many different accounts and didn't know what to believe. The librarian had come up behind her, and Cassie had fobbed her questions off by saying she was doing research for a school project. Everyone seemed to keep a wary eye on Cassie these days.

There was one thing she still needed to do and that was to give her condolences to Todd's father – and ask him some questions. She should have said something to him at the funeral. But he'd looked so odd, so unapproachable, she hadn't wanted to bring on more pain. Her parents had spoken to him since and she knew Jessie would have, somewhere along the line. That she hadn't, nudged her conscience. Todd's father had been in her life for years, albeit on the outer edges, and at times he'd been decent. Now, if the man was computer literate, she'd be more than happy just to send him an e-card or an email. Todd's house was only ten minutes away.

She chewed on her bottom lip, thinking. Fine, ten minutes there and ten minutes back.

***

Deputy Magnusson drove up the long twisting driveway to Martha and Peter's house. He'd known the couple since he was in school. They were different folks. Not for everyone, with Martha being a bit touched in the head. Peter was a good sort. Solid. Not that the young folks of today knew what that meant.

Still, this whole Todd thing seemed to have affected a bunch of kids. He'd had several phone calls this last week asking whether there could be any mistake about the cause of the boy's death. In a way he'd been kinda glad to hear the ruckus. Until one of them had mentioned some writing on some wall on Facebook. He didn't do any social networking. He knew about it, understood the dangers of it, and hated navigating through the mess. He left that crap to his wife and kids who were all die-hard acronym lovers. How did these terms even start? What were some of them? FB, AIM, WOW, COD and then there was something called Twitter, although what that meant he didn't know.

Sometimes he wished the Internet would go down and kids would pick up a hula hoop or play jacks again. He grinned. His kids would hate that. He enjoyed fishing and hiking, even going to lake for the day. His family, on the other hand… Geesh, it took them an hour to load up all the electronic gizmos they had to take with them.

Now Peter was more like him, solid stock from the old days. He parked the truck in front of the house and walked up to the front door. He knocked, yelling out, "Anyone home?"

***

Jessie winced at the sound of his father's truck pulling into the driveway. The garbage can bounced off his bumper as the truck jerked to a stop.

"Mom, Dad's here. And he's drunk, as usual." Jessie continued to eat his dessert, waiting for the upcoming train wreck of events.

The lid of the garbage can shuffled several feet after Adam's heavy boot made hard contact. Jessie sighed as the screen door slammed opened against the side of the house. He'd broken the damn spring years ago. Jessie had fixed it once. There was no point in doing it again. Not when the cause hadn't changed.

Fists pounded on the wooden door.

Jessie watched his mother rush to the door before he dropped his gaze to the last piece of cheesecake on his plate. Some things never changed. His dad was still a drunk and his mom still loved him. He popped the last bite into his mouth and tossed down his fork. Better see what the hell was wrong now.

"Get out of my way," his father's voice roared through the living room.

Jessie frowned and pushed his chair backwards, rising to his feet as his father headed straight for him.

"Adam, what are you doing? Why are you so upset?"

"Hey, Dad? What's up?"

"Don't you 'hey Dad me.'" Jessie's shirt was grabbed, scrunching into Adam's fist. Adam shoved his face into Jessie's. "What the hell were you doing in my house today...yesterday...whenever?" he shouted.

"What?" Jessie reared back as the boozy fumes wafted into his eyes, making them tear up. "Let go of me."

"I'll let go of you when you tell me what you were doing in Todd's bedroom. You were always jealous of your brother." He roared the words, his face blistering red.

"Adam, stop this," Sandra screamed, tugging ineffectually at Adam's hands. "What are you talking about?"

"Him. This lousy rat weasel that went through my house and his brother's room." Adam released Jessie suddenly. Jessie fell back several feet, gasping for breath, his hand on his throat.

Sandra placed herself between the two men. "What are you talking about?"

Jessie should keep his mouth shut – a little hard to do when all he wanted to do was blast the bastard to shreds. "Asshole," he muttered.

"Jessie, stop that," Sandra admonished. "Don't go adding fat to the fire." She turned to Adam. "And you go sit down before you fall down. What do you mean, accusing your son like that?"

"Whaat?" Adam swayed, his hand going out to Sandra's shoulder.

"Come here and sit down." She half-tugged and half-pulled her ex-husband toward the living room. He dropped to the couch, his head bouncing with the force.

Jessie followed at a slower pace, trying to think of an excuse for his presence. The closer to the truth he could get the better. Then again, why not the truth? He had a right to go into the house. His father had always said he was welcome to go visit anytime.

"Now, Adam, please explain." She sat down on the footstool in front of him.

Adam looked around to point at Jessie. "He went through Todd's stuff. Damn thief."

Sandra turned a questioning look on Jessie. "Jessie, is this true?"

Jessie loved the fact that both of his parents had forgotten one thing – that it was supposed to be his home, too. "So what if I did? I thought I was welcome to go anytime. Spend a night, go for a visit. So much for that bullshit."

His mom's face puckered. "There's no need for that type of language."

"Great, he swears and accuses me of stuff, only I can't defend myself in the same way."

"He's not himself," she admonished.

Jessie couldn't believe what he was hearing. "He's what? Not himself? This is who he is! What a joke." He strode across the living room to stand in front of them both. "He's a joke."

"Don't you talk to your father that way? He's a good man."

"He's a drunk." Jessie threw himself down in the single armchair. "Why do you put up with him?"

She shot him a stern look.

Jessie subsided. He glared at his father. "Yes, I went to your house. Sorry, didn't know I was supposed to announce my presence. Oh, except I did but you were passed out as usual."

His father stared at him, total incomprehension on his face.

"Yes, I walked up to Todd's room. I was looking for his cell phone."

"His cell phone?" His mother stared at him in surprise.

"Yes, he didn't have it on him when he was found and there's no sign of it in the burned vehicle."

"Oh, honey. There'd have been nothing left if it had been in the car. What possible difference could it make now?"

"Cassie asked me to look for it."

"Cell phone?" Adam cleared his throat several times. "Todd's phone. He always had it on him."

"I know that. I wondered what had happened to it when it wasn't in the personal effects."

"So what? Surely that wasn't reason enough to search Todd's room."

Jessie shook his head. "I don't believe you two. I'm trying to help and you're both looking at me like I'm a criminal. What a farce." He stood up. "Why don't you just remarry him again? You always take his side anyway."

At the edge of the living room, he tossed back, "And I won't be spending more time with my dad. Right now, I'd be happy never to see him again."

"Wait. Where are you going? Jessie?" His mother's cries rang through the house.

Jessie stormed outside without answering, slamming the front door behind him.

***

Todd watched the interaction in amazement. He'd never seen this side of the family dynamics. Jessie had always figured his life with Dad had been a walk in the park. An easy walk at that. Now he'd seen what a nightmare living with a drunk was. Character building stuff.

A bitter laugh choked out of his silent throat. Too bad they couldn't hear him. He'd love a chance to give them all 'what for.' To remind them what he'd taken for granted – how precious life was. And to tell them they'd been close to being right. He'd probably been heading where they were all afraid he'd been heading.

At least they *would* have been right – if it hadn't been for Cassie.

Just knowing Cassie had been there had kept him on the right path, more often than not. He couldn't bear to disappoint her. Just that adherence to her wishes had stopped him from going too far wrong. He wondered for how long that could have lasted? Maybe not for long, but maybe forever. Impossible to know now.

Todd watched Jessie storm across the yard. Then turned to study his mother as she hovered over his father. His father…well, he appeared to be confused. As usual.

Nothing had changed. His family was still as dysfunctional as ever.

CHAPTER FOURTEEN

Cassie wandered aimlessly around her neighborhood. Adam, Todd's father wasn't at home, so she'd been walking the block, hoping he'd return soon.

"Just go home. You don't need to talk to him, you know."

At the sound of the beloved voice, Cassie turned, a big smile on her face. She was happy to see him, yet sad at the same time. She studied Todd's face. His features were fading slightly, as if his ability to stay here had weakened. That was probably a good thing. He shouldn't be here. He should be off doing whatever dead people did. Hanging around wasn't supposed to be good according to any of the research she'd read. She loved him dearly, but she didn't want him to stay for her or because of the uncertainty clouding the circumstances of his death. She wanted his soul to be at peace and to go wherever souls were supposed to go.

Being trapped here sounded like extending a slow painful death, rather like a crippling disease. Todd was so special, she didn't want to see the essence of what made him who he was, become so much less.

"Whoa, what's with the sad face?" Todd bent forward to peer into her face.

"You." Tears came to her eyes. "You're supposed to be off doing happy soul-like things instead of being stuck here."

"I'm not stuck!" he protested. There went his hands into the jean pockets, his thumbs out as bravado leaked all over. "I'm here because I want to be here."

"Are you," she whispered. "Can you leave anytime?"

"I don't know." He looked around as if afraid someone might hear him. "I'm not sure how to leave, actually. Then, I haven't actually tried, either."

There was something so defenseless, so appealing, so like a young boy who knows he's supposed to do something but doesn't want to – so he makes up stories to get out of it.

"What are you doing here? My dad's at Jessie's. His truck is missing, in case you hadn't realized it," he added helpfully.

She ignored Todd's wicked grin. "Yeah, thanks for pointing out the obvious. I was hoping he'd be here soon."

As she walked to the end of the property, a truck belched around the corner before turning precariously into the driveway.

"I should warn you, he's probably pissed. He had a fight with Jessie."

Cassie stopped abruptly. "He didn't hurt him, did he?"

The whisper of a shrug was barely noticeable. "No, Jessie did all right. Most of the time Dad's okay. Since my accident, well...he needs help."

Cassie snorted. "Personally, I think he needed help a long time ago."

"Yeah, quite possibly. Too bad he wasn't in the car with me. You'd know exactly who was responsible." Disgust laced Todd's tinny voice.

Adam exited the old Dodge pickup, a half empty bottle of Jim Beam swinging from one hand. He slammed the door so hard the whole truck shook. Starting for the house, he stumbled, catching himself before he tumbled face-down on the patchy grass.

Todd's heavy sigh washed over her. "He's got it bad."

She didn't dare answer. She screwed up her courage. "Mr. Spence?"

"What?" Weaving across the lawn to his front door, Adam stared through bloodshot eyes.

It was easiest to start with condolences. "I just wanted to say I'm sorry about Todd." She shrugged. "I really miss him."

He stopped and faced her. "I loved my son. And I've been thinking, it just might have been your fault he's dead."

Cassie gasped, pole-axed. "What?"

Todd stiffened at her side. "That no good lousy drunk!" He headed for his father, fury written all over his face.

Cassie only noted his actions because he came between her and the belligerent drunk in front of her. "I had nothing to do with his death."

"Well, he wouldn't have been out there with his other pals if he'd been with you, now would he?"

Cassie had to sort through that convoluted argument. "You mean I might be responsible because he wasn't with me?" she asked cautiously.

Todd had stopped in his tracks to turn and stare back at her. The matching puzzled looks on both male faces would have been comical if it hadn't been for the seriousness of the subject matter.

"What?" Adam reached up and scratched his head.

Cassie closed her eyes briefly. It was through Adam she'd learned a long time ago that one couldn't talk to a drunk, never mind trying to argue with one.

"Did you see Todd that last night?" she said suddenly.

"Did I? I don't remember."

"Yes, before I went out that night we spoke briefly." Todd supplied the information, studying his father's confused face.

Cassie quickly put that information to use. "I'm sure you must have spoken before he went over to Rob's house to play games that night."

Adam nodded, "Yeah, I think so. I think it was over the phone. That's what I remember."

Cassie took a couple of steps forward. "Maybe you called him that night? Did you ask him to pick up something for you?" She hated the rising tide of hope.

He wavered on the spot as if he couldn't think and stand at the same time. "I called him?"

"No. I'm asking *if* you called him?"

Adam scratched his bristled chin with his truck keys. "I think I talked to him. On the phone."

"Maybe he called you?" She didn't know what difference it made, yet the concept wouldn't leave her alone. Todd had talked to someone on the phone. Someone who'd pissed him off. That put his father at the top of the list.

"Talked to him. Don't know." He shook his head and continued his journey to the front door.

"He called me." Todd frowned at his father. "I remember talking to him."

"Maybe you called him?" Cassie said to Todd softly. At least she thought she'd whispered.

At the front door, Adam turned back. "Huh, what did you say?" He stumbled, grabbing the wall for support.

Cassie groaned softly. "Sorry, I'm just talking to myself." Smiling, Cassie took several steps back toward the driveway. "Good-bye."

Adam half raised the arm holding the booze before letting it drop as he pushed the front door open and fell inside.

"He's too drunk to talk to right now. Call him in the morning, or better, around lunchtime and ask him again. If you want to, that is." Todd fell into step beside her.

"Maybe not. Chances are he'll be too drunk tomorrow to talk, as well." As they walked back to her house, Cassie couldn't stop the feeling that something in that recent conversation was important. It would be normal for Todd to have spoken on the phone with his dad. Most kids did on a daily basis and some on an hourly basis. That didn't feel like the problem, but she couldn't put her finger what was.

As they reached her house, a trip made mostly in silence, she stopped and spun around, looking to ask Todd a question.

Only he'd disappeared – again.

***

Deputy Magnusson strolled around the side of the house, calling out for Peter and Martha. The truck was there. They had to be somewhere. "Martha, are you here?" He stepped up on the back porch and glanced in the glass doors. Martha appeared to be sleeping on the couch. She slept a lot lately. According to the doctors her end was near. As he peered inside, Martha opened her eyes and shrieked.

Gerome held up his hands. "Sorry, Martha. Didn't mean to scare you."

Shaky, Martha sat up, stumbling to her feet before making her way to the door and unlocking it so he could enter. "Sorry, Gerome, I was catching a nap."

"No, it's me who's sorry. I didn't mean to wake you." He walked into the sitting room, watching Martha retake her seat. Sweat beaded on her brow. He winced. "Is Peter around?"

Lying back down, she yawned, covering her mouth with her hand. "I don't know where he's at."

"His truck is parked out front, which is why I walked around back to look for him. Again, I'm sorry. I'll check outside for him." He tilted his head in a respectful nod and backed out.

Martha smiled at him as she lay back down. "Do that. It's nice to see you again."

As he walked away, he noticed a dark blue cell phone lying on the coffee table. That was the same color as Todd's. He couldn't see the brand. He frowned. Martha certainly counted as an old crochety woman, as per Cassie's description of the person who'd answered Todd's phone. Only why wouldn't she have answered when he'd tried to call the number? Walking around to the front of the house again, he called out, "Peter, are you out here?"

Again no answer. Puzzled, he walked to the other side and yelled again. This time he thought he heard a faint moan. He ran around the side of the house to find Peter lying in the deep grass, his left leg crumpled at an odd angle beneath him. Gerome dropped beside him. He quickly realized Peter was barely conscious, his heart racing and uneven.

He needed help and fast. After calling for the ambulance, Gerome took off his jacket and used it to cover the old man up. Too short by half, but it was all he had. Peter's skin had a gray cast, tinged with white.

He needed to let Martha know what had happened, only he didn't want to leave Peter alone. Damn. He made a quick decision and raced up to the back deck where he reopened the glass doors. Martha had fallen asleep again.

"Martha? Martha?" he repeated louder.

She murmured, drifted silent, never lifting her head or opening her eyes.

Damn it. Sirens sounded in the distance. They'd still need a good ten minutes. "Martha?"

This time she hardly moved. Gerome walked in and touched her gently on her shoulder, "Martha, wake up. Peter's hurt." He shook her harder.

Martha's head wobbled and fell to the side, but she didn't open her eyes. Gerome reached a hand to her chilled forehead and frowned. He pressed his fingers to her neck and found only a faint pulse. Her skin felt clammy. She seemed fine ten minutes ago.

Damn it. He needed an ambulance now – for two patients.

He glanced at the cell phone he'd seen earlier. Picking it up, he raced back out to Peter. The older man was still unconscious. Gerome stared down the road. Where the hell was the ambulance?

Opening his wallet, he pulled out a ripped piece of notepaper with a number on it. Using his own phone, he dialed the number. Within seconds the phone in his hand rang. He stared at it in disbelief. Checking the back, he found TS scratched on one corner. Gerome glanced back at the house.

How the hell had Martha ended up with Todd's cell phone?

***

Jessie texted Cassie.

She answered immediately, telling him she'd just returned from trying to talk to his father. Said it hadn't worked out well and she'd try again later.

He snorted. Like that would be effective. His father was drunk now and would be drunk later.

Wanting to hear her voice, he phoned her instead of texting. "Hey, Cassie. Yeah, sorry about Dad. He's not likely to be sober tomorrow, either."

"Maybe, he did mention having talked to Todd on the phone the night he died." Cassie sighed. "I'd hoped to find out what they talked about."

"He spoke with him?"

"Yes, on the phone. At least that's what he said."

"I'll call and talk to him myself in the morning." Jessie checked his watch, realizing he had a few minutes to spare before starting work. "He often calls us, particularly when he's drunk, so that's possible. Still I can't see how this might help."

"It might not. We need to retrace Todd's steps right to the end before we know for sure."

Jessie rubbed the bridge of his nose. "What are you going to do if you find out Todd was the one drinking and driving."

Silence.

Her voice, when it came, was small and painfully honest. "I don't know. I want the truth, only there's always been a small part of me that's afraid of what that is."

"I'm not saying that's what happened, but we may never find out the truth, and that possibility will always be there."

"I know that. I just have to give him every chance first."

Jessie winced at the pain in her voice. "We only have a couple of leads left to follow. After that...well, we'll have to leave it well enough alone."

"I know...and thank you," she whispered. "I need to know I've done everything I can before I walk away."

***

Frustration burst forth. "Walk away. She's going to walk away?" Could she do that? Of course she could. Todd just hadn't thought she would.

A small voice of reason popped up. What had she said? Something about doing everything she could do first before walking away. He hated only getting half a conversation.

"Jessie, I need to get out. My parents aren't home for a while yet, do you want to go for a coffee?"

Jessie? His brother. Instead of raging anger, there was only confusion and...jealousy maybe. That was an unfamiliar sensation. Mixed emotions swept his brain, tiring him. When had his life gotten so confused?

"No, that's okay. I understand. Maybe another time. I'll see you at school tomorrow. Good luck talking to your dad. Don't forget to let me know how it goes."

Todd's emotions fired up and twisted again. Jessie wouldn't meet her for a coffee? What the hell? How dare he? She was a great girl. How could he not go out with her? Just the concept pissed him off. Didn't Jessie know how special Cassie was? He should've been jumping for joy at being asked.

Belatedly, he realized Cassie was still talking to Jessie. "Have a good evening at work. Yeah. Later."

Shit. Jessie was on his way to work. Todd groaned. He was losing it. He'd shifted from being jealous that Jessie was talking to Cassie, to being pissed that Jessie wouldn't meet her and now he was relieved that Jessie *couldn't* meet Cassie, not that he wouldn't. He was a mess. A dead mess.

"Todd, hi! I've missed you." Her beaming smile as she saw him and put away her phone warmed him inside, easing the edgy emotions. His sigh of relief was heartfelt. She loved him.

He knew that and he also knew she needed some people in her life. Good people. And if he couldn't be there for her, and he'd given it an almighty try to remain longer, then, he had to admit that Jessie might be the right guy to take his place.

***

The hospital never seemed to go into quiet mode. The sun went to bed, the moon rose and fell, yet the hospital always hummed with activity.

Gerome, hat in hand, hovered. He couldn't help it. There was nothing like seeing a group of industrious people moving to a silent orchestra that only they could hear. They did it with musical precision, making him feel useless.

Martha and Peter were both in Emergency, being worked on by separate teams. Gerome had no idea if either, or both would survive. He'd contacted his boss and brought him up to speed on the situation. Sheriff Lance Donner was a good man and even he realized the cell phone issue needed to be clarified. There was no way to know when that could happen, given the craziness going on now.

"Deputy, please move down to the waiting room. You're in the way," scolded one nurse on her third pass around him.

Gerome looked around the room and realized there was no place to get out of the way without leaving. The same nurse stopped, grabbed his arm and turned him in the direction of the seats. "Down there." She gave him a little push on his ample shoulders. "Go, now."

He gave her a goofy grin and headed over to sit. He waited. He got coffee, pondering the cell phone. He'd taken a moment to check the calls on Todd's phone while he could and there'd been a few. At this point, he didn't know if any were important. The ambulance had arrived then and he'd raced out to follow.

Finally a doctor walked over to him.

"Deputy?"

Gerome struggled to his feet. "Doctor Robinson. How are they?"

The doctor studied Gerome's face. "It's a good thing you were there, Deputy. Peter's going to be fine only we're going to keep him and run some tests. His pulse is too low and he's still in shock. As for Martha, well, her time has come. We're hoping Peter wakes up so he can see her before she's gone, except if he doesn't wake up soon...I think he'll be too late."

"She's been sick a long time." Gerome knew it would be hard on Peter any time. It would be harder still if he didn't get a chance to say good-bye.

"Yes, she has, and she's come to the end of the road. Not to worry, we'll make her as comfortable as possible."

"Is she awake? Any chance I could ask her a few questions?"

"No. And she's not likely to wake again."

Gerome pursed his lips. It's what he'd figured. "What about Peter?"

"Now he *might* be able to talk in a bit. They're still getting him stabilized. His leg is going to need to be set and the cardiologist needs to see him. He just might need a pacemaker before he leaves the hospital."

"A pacemaker?"

"Depending on the test results. With his pulse dropping like it did...that could be next. The cardiologist will decide. Why don't you go home? Call the nurses' station for an update before you come back."

"Thanks, I'll do that."

"Don't forget, he's liable to be pretty emotional over Martha already, so try not to upset him. That will cause heart trouble he can't afford, in his condition."

"Understood." With a final nod, Gerome headed to the nurses' station to request a call when Peter was able to talk. Then he would head home. On his way out, the dispatcher called. Another car accident.

So much for dinner tonight.

CHAPTER FIFTEEN

Tuesday really sucked once she logged onto her Facebook account and saw a message from Todd.

It couldn't be from Todd. Not unless he'd found a way to communicate electronically. And even then, he'd have told her himself. Some jerk had to be using his account. Why? To scare her? To make her wonder if Todd had really died? His coffin had been closed. She never did see Todd's body. She grimaced. Like who'd want to?

Using his account to stir up trouble? Now that was low.

Pissed, and with all that hurt to deal with, crabbiness ruled while she finished dressing and headed downstairs. Giving a perfunctory smile to her mother who stood at the stove, she strode right out the door.

"Aren't you going to eat breakfast, Cassie?"

Cassie let the door slam behind her, ignoring her mother's question. She didn't want breakfast. She only wanted peace.

As she approached the place she usually met Penny, she wasn't surprised to find there was no sign of her, either. Had someone sent her a message from Todd, too?

Cassie kicked a rock the rest of the way to the school, wanting to release some of the anger inside.

"What's the matter, Cassie?"

"Missing your boyfriend, Cassie? Need a new boy toy for some fun?"

Brodie and Aric had come up behind her. Great. She'd hoped she was done with these two. Yet if they wanted a fight today, well, they could have it.

"I don't want to talk to you two. Go away."

"Go away." Aric snorted. "Like we have to listen to you."

"No, you don't have to, but you will. Like I want anything to do with you."

"And what's wrong with us?" asked Aric, indignantly.

She slid him a disgusted look. "What's right with you?"

He came to a halt. "Hey, be nice."

She spun around to walk backwards. "Don't be an idiot. You spend all your time trying to frighten and intimidate everyone. Who's going to like you, except Brodie and Dory?"

"We do not," he blustered. "Everyone likes me."

Brodie sent a silent dark look at Aric. "Don't be an idiot."

Aric subsided with a dirty look at Cassie.

The school gates appeared in front of them. Cassie strode through. Aric fell in behind. At the stairs, Cassie twisted to look behind her. Brodie stood at the gate, his arms crossed, glaring at her.

"What's the matter with your friend?" Cassie motioned behind her.

Aric shrugged. "He's having a bad day. Someone sent him an email from Todd's account. He's pissed about it."

Cassie stopped mid-stride and grabbed his arm. "What did you say?"

"You heard me," he muttered. "And don't tell him I said so."

"You don't understand. I got one, too."

"No shit?"

"Yes. It was there this morning. That's why I was so nasty. It pissed me off. I know it could be just a harmless joke, only it feels nastier. If you hadn't said that about Brodie, I'd have thought the email was his work."

"No. Besides he's not geeky like that. Only knows the basics."

"Well, someone hacked Todd's account to cause trouble. I, for one, don't know anyone who'd be good enough, except Todd himself."

Todd had been a natural-born hacker and lacked the willingness to apply the same dedication to the proper education channels. He'd taken computer science last year, only arguments with the teacher had resulted in getting booted from class. His mark had been in the high nineties. He could have fought it and continued, except Todd had a problem with authority. Cassie realized in hindsight, Todd hadn't liked much about school. Yet he would have graduated.

Now she wondered what he'd have done in six weeks when school had finished. What could he have done? Continued to work at the store? He'd hated that job.

Todd had been brilliant. But not challenged.

So who felt they were better than he was? Who felt they needed to best Todd, even after he was dead. Who wanted to show everyone they could?

***

Gerome entered the front doors of the hospital the next morning. He hadn't had a chance to come back last night. He needed to ask a few questions. Like where the cell phone had come from.

"Hey, Peter, you're looking better." Peter's skin had a pink flush, only the whites of his eyes showed a yellow sallowness that made Gerome wince. Peter had never been a big man, but now he really looked gaunt and thin. These last months had been tough on him.

Peter opened his eyes to stare at him. After a moment, recognition flashed. "Thanks for coming by when you did. I guess you saved my life." Peter reached up a hand to grab Gerome's.

Squeezing his hand gently, Gerome grinned at his old friend. "I don't know about that. I'm sure someone would have come by eventually."

Peter coughed. "I don't think so. I'd been there for quite a while." His fingers moved restlessly on the sheets. "Thanks for helping Martha, too."

"I'm sure sorry about her condition." Gerome grabbed the room's single chair and pulled it closer before sitting down.

Peter watched him, bleak acceptance in his eyes. "Don't be. They tell me she's unconscious and won't likely wake up. It's better this way." He sighed and rested back. "She's had a few tough years, that old gal. She's been a good 'un."

"Still, it's hard."

Peter nodded slightly, his old eyes shining wetly. "Aye, it is."

Gerome said, "Peter, when I was at your place and talking to Martha, I saw a cell phone on the coffee table. It belongs to a young man who died just over a week ago."

Peter's gaze widened. "Really?"

"He was killed in a car accident at the corner just past your house."

Using his elbows, Peter rolled over slightly so he could see Gerome. "I remember that accident. A couple of kids wandered the site later."

Cassie. That would be something she'd do. "Where'd you get the phone from?"

"I picked it up a while back when I collected the mail from the box. The phone lay off to one side. I thought maybe it belonged to the mailman. I asked him the next day, only he didn't know anything about it." Peter stared up at the ceiling. "So, I figured someone had pulled off to the side of the road and lost it getting in or out of the car."

"When did you find it?"

"Let me think." He worked his fingers, counting days. "I think it was the Monday after the accident. Not likely later than that. It never occurred to me to that it was related to the boy."

"Did you ever use the phone?"

"Me? Naw. I don't like them things. Got a perfectly good phone at home, why would anyone want one to stick a phone in their pocket? So folks could bug the hell out of you some more?"

Gerome grinned. "Would Martha have answered it if it rang?"

"Martha? Yes. I took the battery out 'cause it was wet, and when I put it back in, she said the darn thing woke her up. So I took it out again until it had dried." He straightened his sheet again. "She was pretty foggy these last weeks, though, so she wouldn't have made a lick of sense, even if she did answer."

Gerome stood up. "I'll let you rest now. Thanks for taking the time to talk to me. I'll try to stop by tomorrow." He turned to leave, then stopped. "If Martha wakes up, give her my best."

"I will." Peter shuffled upward on his bed. "Thanks for stopping by."

"Any time, old friend...any time."

***

Jessie texted Cassie on her way home from school. She read it and grinned. He'd talked to his dad on the phone. Apparently Adam had called Todd that last night and asked him to go to the liquor store.

"Like that's going to happen. Todd wasn't old enough to buy booze. His father knew that." Thankfully no one was around as she talked to the air again. Cassie remembered seeing the broken glass at the accident site and a torn, charred label. The same label as the one she'd seen on the bottle in Adam's hands earlier.

"Now that I think of it, that makes total sense. That's why there was booze in the vehicle. He'd gone shopping for his dad. Except as he couldn't buy it himself, there had to be someone with him." Wow. Cassie immediately called Jessie back. "Hey, Jessie. Did he say anything else?"

"Not really. Just that Todd hadn't wanted to go to the liquor store since he was on his way home…but according to Adam, he'd finally agreed to."

Cassie pounced. "Todd was on his way home?"

"Right. That's what dad said?" Jessie spoke slowly now.

"So that's the last thing Todd did before the accident. There wasn't enough time for much else. He dropped off his friends, went to the liquor store and connected with someone who bought the booze for him. Your dad has to know who that was."

"Was there time for someone else to get into the picture?" Jessie's voice strengthened forcefully. "We have to be honest here. There is the chance that Todd drank some of that alcohol himself and then drove home. If he'd had something before or while he was gaming with his friends then more afterwards…"

Silence.

Cassie closed her eyes, desperately wanting to erase those words that hung so heavily between them. "No. I don't have to be that honest," she whispered, painfully.

"Cassie, I know you feel that way. I just don't want you to be hurt if it turns out differently."

"I know that. Let's return to the main topic. How can we find out who bought the booze?"

"We could ask the deputy to question whoever was working at the liquor store that night? He might do that."

"Maybe?" Cassie didn't know that he would though; she'd been sending emails pretty often and he didn't always reply. He was probably sick of her. "Not that this case is a priority."

"Maybe not, but that doesn't mean he wouldn't follow up, at our request."

"True." Cassie thought about the options. Her house loomed ahead. "So stop by tomorrow after school, send the deputy an email or what?"

"An email he'd get in the morning. I don't have his cell phone number and am not sure that I'm comfortable calling him at his house, even if we had the number." Jessie's warm teasing voice sounding through the phone, made her toes curl.

Since when had Jessie's voice felt like warm hug? Cassie shook her herself. Her head was hooked way too much on this guy. He'd infiltrated her mind and even her dreams. She sighed heavily. What a lost cause.

"Cassie? Are you okay?"

Never. "I'm fine." She shook her head gently. "Just thinking. I'm going to do both. I'll email him tonight and I can go by his office after school."

"Not alone."

Cassie stopped and looked at her phone. "What?"

"I'd like to come with."

"Oh." Her toes wiggled.

"If you don't mind." Now Jessie's voice deepened with insecurity.

Rushing the last few feet, Cassie burst inside and upstairs to her room. "No. Sorry. That's fine." She laughed. "That's great, actually." She walked over to her bedroom window and stared out. "I didn't think you'd want to come."

He was quiet for a long moment. "I'd really like a chance to get to know you better." His voice deepened yet again. "If you're interested, that is."

Opening the window, Cassie leaned against the frame, breathing in the fresh air, a warm smile curling up her insides. She grinned. "I'm interested." Cassie laughed again feeling heat rush over her face and tickle her toes.

She couldn't keep the silly smile off her face for the rest of the afternoon.

***

Jessie hung up his phone, grinning like a clown on drugs. "Well, that went well."

His mom poked her head in his room. "Did you say something, honey?"

"No, I was talking to a friend on the phone."

She took one look at his face and smirked. "And to a girl from the looks of it."

"What?" Jessie glanced down at the closed phone in his hands then slipped it into his pocket.

"I said that you were obviously speaking with a girl. A special one, if that look is anything to go by?"

He looked down at the floor, and kicked out his foot aimlessly.

She laughed. "That's fine. I won't tease you about her – at least not too much."

Jessie rolled his eyes. "Oh great."

"I wanted to know if you're working tomorrow after school?"

"Uhmm. No, not until Wednesday."

"Good. Can I get you to stop by the accountant's and pick up some papers for me?"

"I can do that. Well, maybe. What time do I need to get them?"

"Before four. That's why I'm asking you. I can't get there in time. Although, I might be able to run over at lunchtime."

Jessie shook his head. The accountant's office wasn't far away from the sheriff's. He could go both places in decent time. "No, don't worry about it. It should be fine. Cassie won't mind stopping."

"Cassie?"

Jessie frowned at the sharp tone and narrowed his eyes. Now what was she all hot and bothered about? "Yeah, Cassie. What's the matter, Mom?"

"I don't know if I should mention this, but..." She straightened her shoulders. "I feel I should say something. I'm a little worried about you spending time with that girl."

Huh, oh. "That girl?"

"Todd's girlfriend. Cassie."

"What about her?" Jessie shifted to lean against his bedroom door. He would prefer to avoid this discussion, except he knew his mother too well. If she didn't say what was on her mind, she'd keep at it and at it.

"I just think you should avoid her, that's all."

"That's all? You need to elaborate, Mom. Why should I?"

"For one, she was Todd's girlfriend. You need to get your own. For another, I'm not sure if she didn't have a negative effect on Todd's character. All that drinking, skipping school and the carousing he did."

Only his mother could put skipping school in the middle of those offenses. "I think you misunderstand. Cassie and Todd were friends. Not boyfriend and girlfriend. Not lovers. They didn't drink together, nor did they carouse together, as you put it. They were friends – and only friends."

"I know you believe that."

"No, Mom. I know that."

"What? You and she haven't...?" She stared at him in shock.

Jessie's eyes widened. "What? No. No. I...we... haven't. No!"

Her hand patted her chest in relief, her face turning bright red. "Oh, thank heavens. Well, that's good. Good." She looked everywhere but at him. "Okay. I won't mention that again."

She turned and hurried away.

***

"Cassie, I understand you talked to Dr. Sanchez the other day?"

Cassie's fork stopped in mid-air. She stared at what been a decent lasagna before her mother had opened her mouth. Slowly she put the bite in her mouth, refusing to look at either of the two adults staring covertly at her. She chewed, thinking about what to say. She swallowed finally, and nodded her head. "Yes, I did."

She almost laughed at the relief washing over both their faces. Determinedly, she forked in another bite and waited. Her mother had no patience.

"And?"

Cassie looked up innocently. "And what?"

"How did it go?" Her father jumped in, his voice brusque. "Did you talk to her?"

"Yes, she was just about to leave for the day." Cassie popped more lasagna into her mouth, watching them exchange looks. They couldn't just come out and ask. They always tiptoed around topics. She considered what she wanted to tell them. Not much, obviously, as she hadn't told them about stopping in there in the first place.

"Look. I stopped in. She was there, and so we talked for a few minutes. No big deal, okay?"

"Honey, we're just happy that you went at all."

Cassie rolled her eyes and kept eating.

"When are you going to see her next?"

Playing with her fork instead of eating, Cassie considered whether she'd rather get up and leave or eat a little more. If they kept up the questioning, she'd leave. "I don't know that I am."

Her father's fork dropped to the table as he glared at her over his empty plate. "Why not?"

"Tom," murmured Abby, giving him a warning look.

Cassie put her fork down. "Thanks for dinner, Mom." She got up, picked up her plate – still half-full – and headed into the kitchen.

"Remember, she said not to push."

Her mom's harsh whisper filtered through to the kitchen, loud and clear.

Tom's brusque voice followed. "What? Can't I even ask her anything anymore?"

"Not if it's going to upset her. We don't want to stop her from going."

Abby kept her voice quiet. Tom didn't care. "You're babying her. So what if her friend died? People die all the time. It's time she grew up and started being mature about all of this."

"Tom, that's not nice."

Cassie tuned out her parents' squabbling. Personally, she felt she'd grown up a lot lately. Too bad the adults around her hadn't.

CHAPTER SIXTEEN

Cassie found it hard to focus the next morning. There'd been another posting 'from Todd' on her Facebook page. *Greetings from the world of the undead.* And as much as she'd like to block the sender, it was Todd's original account and she couldn't quite bring herself to do that – because it was also so close to the truth of his predicament that it just added to her pain.

There were any number of people capable of finding out Todd's account name and password but the ones she'd considered wouldn't care to. That's what she didn't understand. Why bother? To upset her? It was succeeding. Yet that had more to do with the shock of seeing his name than anything else. If the person was out to cause mischief, it was pretty minor.

Jessie stood at the school gates, casually talking to a couple of his friends. Cassie's heart sped up. She hated blushing, but knew when he looked at her that her face was turning pink. She chastised herself for it. She'd seen him lots. Had been getting to know him for a while now. He was Todd's brother, for heaven's sake. What was wrong with her?

"It's different now," she whispered under her breath. "Everything's different."

"Not really."

Cassie spun to see Todd walking on her heels. Her face lit up, until she realized she was being watched. "You're getting me into so much trouble," she muttered under her breath.

"You're getting yourself in trouble." His grin was contagious.

Not this time. She glared at him. Realizing a stranger walking behind her was staring back at her, she flushed bright red. "Sorry," she muttered and stalked past the collection of curious onlookers.

"Cassie, wait up."

Cassie quickened her pace. She didn't know who'd called but she wanted to escape.

"Cassie?" Jessie loped beside her. "What's your hurry?"

Slowing down slightly, Cassie smiled. "Sorry, I thought I was late for class." She glanced around. There was no sign of Todd.

"No. It's still early yet. You've got at least five minutes."

She didn't know what to say. Five minutes in her world wasn't much, only guys seemed to view it as a long time. "I have to go to my locker yet. Are we still on for this afternoon?"

The dark depths of his eyes lit up. "Absolutely." The light dimmed as he added, "And I have to run by the accountant's and pick up some papers for my mom. The office is on the way."

"No problem." Cassie didn't mind. A little longer in his company was a good thing.

"Good."

They stopped at her locker, looking at each other. He shifted awkwardly, stuffing his hands into his pockets. Cassie unlocked her locker, opening it to pull out her English book. Reaching up one arm, Cassie tucked a few loose strands of hair behind her ear and blew out her breath. The school bell rang.

Cassie smiled, relieved. "Until later."

***

Adam reached for the bottle and raised it to his lips. He wanted a drink. He wanted it really badly. And it was there. In front of him.

Yet he couldn't seem to take a drink.

Guilt consumed him, didn't allow him to sleep, eat or, apparently, to drink anymore. Drinking had helped him to forget. He wanted forgetfulness. He needed it. It was the only way he could get through his day. Through the nightmare his life had become. It had been bad before. His life on a downward spiral after he'd hit that poor woman.

Guilt.

Guilt that he might have contributed to his son's death.

Guilt that he might have killed his boy outright.

Guilt that he might have snuffed out the only good thing in his life.

Tears started streaming down his face.

He wiped them away.

They wouldn't stop. He grabbed his sleeve and wiped, then wiped again. Tears continued to fall. Adam's heart broke, one teardrop at a time. Within minutes he cried in earnest and, like a baby, he curled up on his side and bawled. The tempest lasted hours. When it passed, he cuddled up into a ball and fell asleep.

***

Cassie couldn't wait for the last class of the morning to finally end. The whole day had appeared endless. Absolute torture. The teachers just wouldn't shut up. In contrast, lunch hour resembled a cyclone, whipping past her in a blur. Penny had asked about Jessie, unleashing giggles and girl talk – a welcome relief from the intense waiting sensation.

"So are you going to see him again?"

Cassie looked sideways at Penny. They both giggled.

"This afternoon."

"Ooooh." Penny leaned toward Cassie, peering around at the others. "Are you going on a date?"

Cassie smirked. Keeping her voice down, she replied, "No, we're just going to walk home together."

"Wow, does he live close to you?"

"Not really. About fifteen minutes away from Todd's place."

"How would Todd handle this?"

Cassie stopped, straightened up and stared at her best friend. How *would* Todd feel about this? She searched the room, afraid Todd was staring down at her in disgust. Thankfully, he wasn't there.

"I don't know. Todd and I were friends. We weren't boyfriend-girlfriend kind of friends. Everyone thought we were, only we weren't."

"I know you've said that in the past, but I did kinda wonder."

Cassie closed her eyes and shook her head. "No. Todd and I were close, really close. We loved each other, just not like that. That's why he had girlfriends. We used to talk about his relationships and why he chose those kinds of girls. We used to laugh about the guys I had crushes on. In fact, Todd used to make suggestions as to which guys were okay and which ones to avoid. You remember. I used to tell you about some of them?"

Penny sat up straight. "Yes, I do." She studied Cassie's smiling face. "Do you really think he'd be okay with you going out with his brother?"

"Well, I'm not going out with him exactly, just getting to know him better."

Penny giggled.

Cassie laughed. "Stop it. We're just, you know...friends."

That set Penny off giggling again, and Cassie had to admit it was pretty funny. In a party mood once again, the two girls headed back toward PE class, first up in the afternoon. Pushing through the crowd, the girls walked happily toward the gym.

Cassie gasped when she was suddenly slammed up against the lockers. A strong arm pressed against her neck; a knee, and hip pinned her to the metal.

Kendra.

"Leave her alone, you witch." Penny pulled on Kendra's arm as Cassie struggled to get loose, only Kendra was several years older, taller and heavier. Not to mention meaner.

"Lay off. Todd was mine, and Jessie will never be yours."

"What the...?"

"Did you hear me, you bitch?" Kendra snarled.

Cassie choked and coughed. Kendra eased the pressure against her throat.

"What is your problem, Kendra? You ruined your relationship with Todd, and you're dreaming if you think his brother will give you the time of day."

"Bitch. I didn't do anything wrong with Todd. I loved him. It's your fault our relationship didn't last. You put a wedge between us." Kendra's bitterness boiled over, releasing months of anger and pain.

Cassie stared at her in astonishment. "You're full of it. You slept with his friend. You slept with Levine." Cassie remembered Todd's reaction when Levine had confessed. Even though there'd been little in the way of love between Todd and Kendra, he'd been hurt by the betrayal. Cassie never understood if it was Levine's betrayal or Kendra's that had hurt Todd the most.

Kendra eased up more. "He wouldn't have told you that. He couldn't have. He loved me."

Cassie mocked her. "Loved you? Like hell. You cheated on him, betrayed him. You destroyed any feelings he had for you." She shrugged Kendra off, slipping out from under her arm. "How dare you say you loved him? You loved yourself. You used him." Cassie took several steps toward the gym, pulling Penny with her. "Now leave me alone. The next time you pull a stunt like that I'll report you."

"Go ahead. No one will believe you. They're already saying you're losing it. That Todd's death has affected you in the head."

Suddenly Cassie had had it. Tired of Kendra's crap. Tired of trying to figure out what had happened. Tired of trying to hold it all together. She just didn't care anymore. "What's the matter,

Kendra, guilt eating away at you? Are you the one using Todd's Facebook account to send out emails? Wanting to keep Todd close, you hijacked his account. How pathetic is that? Todd never loved you. He screwed you – until you screwed him by cheating on him. Then he couldn't even be bothered to do that anymore."

Kendra's face bristled, her eyes darkening to black. "How dare you! Todd loved me. I made the memorial page to honor him, because he loved me. Me. Not you. He didn't give you his account information, did he? I didn't have to hijack anything. He gave me his password a long time ago."

"Right. Pillow talk? Did you pass that information on to Levine too? How about Isaac? Or Michael?"

Fury darkened Kendra's face.

"Wow, momma. You may have gone too far." Penny backed up, pulling Cassie's arm. "Come on. Let's get out of here."

Cassie stood her ground and faced Kendra down. Built like an exotic dancer with pink hair, Kendra was a mean enemy. If Cassie didn't finally beat Kendra at her own game, there'd be no end of this day-in and day-out bullying. "Do you really think everyone doesn't know, Kendra? You sleep with anyone for a drink. For a meal. For a laugh."

Tears sprang to Kendra's eyes. Though Cassie felt mean, she didn't dare back down. Kendra had to face reality. "You are no one to me, yet Todd was everything to both us. Too bad only one of us respected him and his love."

"That's not true," Kendra whispered heavily, her lithe body sagging against the lockers and slowly sliding down to the floor. Tears welling in the corner of her eyes. "I loved him."

"Yeah, you might have. At least you loved him as you much as you know how. You had a chance at something wonderful. You blew it."

"I didn't know until it was too late." Kendra wiped her eyes with the back of her hands. "I'd never had a guy treat me right and so I never–"

"Treated them right." Cassie finished for her, staring down at the scuffed up hallway floor. "Well, you were gifted with someone who would have done well by you. Maybe you will learn from this."

"And Jessie?" Kendra asked bitterly.

"Forget Jessie. He won't touch Todd's leftovers."

Kendra snorted. Her voice cuttingly sarcastic as she snapped, "Yet you think he'll be willing to touch you."

Cassie stiffened. Penny's grip on her arm tightened. "Why not," she said coolly. "I'm not one of Todd's leftovers, and Jessie already knows it." She'd have laughed at the look on Kendra's face any other time, but this conversation was too painful and too brutal for humor.

With a last commiserating smile in Kendra's direction, Cassie and Penny raced to class, leaving Kendra to nurse her wounds.

***

Jessie knew the rumors had been distorted but would be loosely based on fact. What he heard made him both wince and grin. That Todd's girlfriend should have played so fast and loose was comically sad, particularly considering Todd was dead. He personally didn't think his brother would have cared about Kendra's behavior. He'd probably thought it was funnier than hell. Taking what he wanted from the relationship and giving nothing back.

The part of the rumor involving him made for interesting pondering. Should he ask Cassie about it this afternoon or leave well enough alone?

Maybe she'd mention it herself.

Jessie waited at the front steps for Cassie to show up. He'd planned to go to the accountant's first. He glanced at his watch.

She wasn't late yet. There were still a lot of teens milling around the area. Cassie should be along any minute.

"Waiting for your girlfriend, Jessie?" The laughter and jokes surrounded him. He took it all in stride, feeling a secret warmth at the concept. He wished. He could only hope that Cassie would want the position. He could certainly understand Todd's attraction.

At the reminder of his brother, his stomach cooled. A new worry crept in. Was he stealing Todd's girlfriend? Not really – after all, Todd was dead. He couldn't be here with her anymore.

Yet he felt like he was overstepping an invisible boundary.

"Well, brother. I don't know what to say. You're not here anymore. She's lonely, interested and, well, I'm here and you're not. I wouldn't be doing this if you were still alive."

Kids came through the doors and scrambled down the stairs for freedom. A weird feeling of being watched came over him. He spun around. He studied the faces of the few people standing around also waiting for friends or rides to appear. No one appeared to notice him.

Still, he couldn't rid of the feeling that someone watched him.

***

He followed Jessie outside.

"Why can't you hear me, you stupid idiot? You know how much easier it would be if you'd listen. Then, you never listened to me when I was alive, so why would you now?" Todd sat down on the cement steps and leaned back against a cement wall. Only four feet separated him from his brother, though it might as well have been four miles.

Cassie walked out the front door of the school directly in front of Todd and Jessie.

"Hi, Cassie." Todd waved at her, happy to have someone to talk to. A big grin crossed her face as she came toward him. Cassie came to a sudden halt and Todd understood that she'd now seen him…and Jessie. Her smile came again, this time warm and intimate and directed his way. Todd's heart warmed. "Hi, kiddo. Are you meeting my brother?"

Her smile brightened and she gave an almost imperceptible nod and turned a bit. "Hi, Jessie. Are you ready?"

"Yeah. I wasn't sure if you'd stood me up."

"Stood you up?" Geesh. He doesn't know you at all, does he?" Todd grinned at the dirty look Cassie shot him.

She reached down and caught Jessie's arm, tugging him upright. "If you knew me better you'd know that wouldn't happen. At least, not unless it was an emergency."

Jessie wrapped an arm around her shoulders and headed down the stairs with her. Todd watched them walk off, laughing together. At the school gates, Cassie turned once to look behind her.

Todd waved. She beamed a smile at him, before walking away.

Todd had never felt so lonely. At the same time, a sense of rightness enveloped him. This was a good thing for Cassie. A sense of completeness hovered at his shoulder. It wasn't quite time yet, only now he knew that when the time was right, he'd be able to leave. Soon.

CHAPTER SEVENTEEN

Cassie felt like the clock had turned backwards. Laughter and joy filled her heart and warmth filled her veins. Now if only she could stop sighing with happiness every few minutes. She had to sound like complete idiot.

Jessie was so funny. He was a lot like Todd, yet he was his own special self. She no longer accidentally saw Todd in his face. She knew Jessie well enough now to see him for who *he* was. Her heart no longer wanted to see Todd in Jessie.

She glanced upward and smiled. Jessie squeezed her arm. "Here we are."

Jessie tugged the door open and let Cassie go in first. At the reception area, Cassie asked, "Could we see Deputy Magnusson, please?"

"I don't know if he's in. I can go check. Please take a seat."

"Thanks. He should be expecting us." The woman nodded and left.

Cassie and Jessie wandered the small room. Cassie didn't want to sit down. She didn't want to stay very long. This should be a quick stop before dragging Jessie off to try coffee again.

Todd slipped into her mind. She grimaced. That had been too weird coming out of the school and seeing the two of them sitting together like that. Jessie'd had no idea. It had taken a lot of effort to avoid looking like a total moron in front of Jessie, without hurting Todd. This talking to empty air stuff was making her look like a nutcase. Then she remembered Kendra's comment and sighed. She didn't need any more comments like that.

An oak door opened on the side wall. Cassie turned to see Deputy Magnusson waiting for her. "Hi again, Cassie. You like to keep your word, I see. That's good. Come on into my office." His eyebrows raised as Jessie stepped up to her side. "You must be Todd's brother."

Jessie stepped forward. "Yes, sir." He held out his hand to shake. "I'm Jessie. Todd was my older brother."

"Come on in."

Once in the small office, Cassie and Jessie took seats. Cassie looked at the deputy. "Deputy, the Facebook issue has been solved. I'm sorry for disturbing you on that account."

"What was that about?"

"One of Todd's old girlfriends knew his account and password and used it to send messages from the dead. More for shock value than anything else."

"Malicious."

"Yes, only she was hurting, and lashed out."

The deputy pondered her face for a long moment before nodding. "Good, that's one issue resolved. I also found Todd's cell phone."

Cassie jumped to her feet. "Oh, that's excellent. Where was it?"

"It was dumped, lost, or dropped on a driveway across the road from where the accident took place." He opened the file on his desk, shuffling through the pages, obviously looking for something.

Tilting her head, Cassie had to consider that news for a moment. "At the old man's house?"

The deputy nodded. "Anyway, we searched the records and there's nothing that indicates another person connected with Todd that night, outside of his father, that is."

"We know his father called. He said he asked him to make a liquor store run." Cassie paused and shifted her gaze to Jessie. "The thing is, Todd wasn't old enough to buy booze, and so we don't know if he ever did. Or whether someone he knew bought it for him, and therefore could have been the last person to see him alive that night." She took another deep breath. This was it. "We wondered if you could talk to the staff on duty that night and see if they saw anything." The words just gushed out. "They might be able to identify Todd and who he was with."

The deputy sighed and leaned back.

"I know we're asking a lot. And that we have already asked a lot of you. Please. This one more thing. This one more conversation to make sure we haven't missed anything? Surely, it's important to know if the liquor store is selling to underage kids?" she wheedled. "Todd's cell phone didn't make it to the top of that hill on its own." Cassie leaned forward. "Please," she added, "he was a good kid and he deserves for us to try this one more thing."

The deputy jotted down something on a piece of paper. "You are a very persistent young lady."

She gave him her most winning smile. "I'm also a very loyal friend."

Deputy Magnusson glanced between their two hopeful faces, then sighed. "If I do this one last thing we put this to rest. Got it?"

In unison, they both cried, "Got it."

***

Jessie looked at Cassie once they made it back out to the sidewalk. "That went well."

"Yeah, I guess," she said in an uncertain voice. Cassie linked arms with him in a natural movement that made him smile. A special warmth unfurled inside.

Jessie frowned. What was bothering her now? "What's the matter? Don't you think he'll follow up on the liquor store?"

They started to walk toward the soda shop. "I'm sure he will try." Cassie kicked a rock off the sidewalk. "I'm just impatient. I want him to go now, and I want to be there so I can hear the answers and know the right questions were asked."

"You have to let him do his job, Cassie. He knows how to do this better than you do."

"I know that." Cassie pushed the button to cross the intersection. "I just want this over with."

The light changed and she stepped onto the road. Just as they reached the other side, Jessie's phone went off. Fishing it out of his pocket, he answered his mom's call. "Hi. I already picked up the papers." He glanced down at Cassie. "Dad? What about him? He's probably just sleeping off another bender."

"I don't think so. I have a horrible feeling, honey. I can't reach him. I've been trying all day. I can't get away from work. Would you mind checking on him?"

Oh no. Why today? Why now? Jessie glanced around, getting his bearings. "I guess I can. I'm not that far away."

"Please call me back when you get there."

"Yeah." Jessie rolled his eyes at Cassie, who stood watching, one eyebrow raised as though she was wondering what was happening.

"I can do that."

Jessie tucked the phone back in his pocket. "Sorry, Cassie, I have to cancel out on coffee. I have to go and check on my dad. Mom's been trying to reach him all day and she's worried."

Understanding flitted across her face. "I can see how he'd be worrisome. Come on, let's go."

"You don't have to come with me. He's not much fun to be around." Except Jessie didn't want to break off his time with her.

"Maybe not, but I'm not going to avoid him because of that. Let's get our coffees to go. We'll stop by his house, then go on to mine for a bit, later."

Jessie grinned. "Perfect."

***

Adam's truck was parked at an angle in the driveway. The curtains were closed like they'd been every other time she passed by since the accident. The front grass stood a foot high. A horrible deserted feeling permeated the house.

Cassie shivered. "He's really not doing well since losing Todd, is he?"

Jessie glanced at her quickly. "No, he's not. I've never seen him as bad as he's been this last couple of weeks."

"The death of a child will do that, I suppose." Especially given a pre-existing weakness like alcoholism, only Jessie didn't need to be reminded of that. She studied Jessie's face. He hadn't had it easy these last weeks, either, dealing with his weak mother, weaker father and the loss of his brother. He was holding up well, turning into a man in front of her. The younger brother was now fast becoming the head of the family.

She'd been more than willing to lean on him herself.

Jessie strode up to the front door and rang the doorbell. The two waited. There was no sound from inside.

"Try again? Push the door open and call out?" Cassie suggested.

"The last time I went in without his knowledge he blew up at me, accusing me of all kinds of things, including stealing. So I don't want to go in without his permission, yet if there's something wrong with him..." Jessie let his voice trail off as he pounded harder on the door, only to have it fall open under his fist.

"Well, we don't have to worry about it being locked."

"He never locks it." As if gathering his courage, Jessie stood for a quick moment, then pushed the door wide open and walked in. Cassie followed. No lights brightened the dim room and no amount of shadows could hide the dismal sight. Cassie winced at the bottles, garbage and the stench... She almost gagged.

"What is that smell?"

"Booze, piss and rotting garbage, probably."

Piss? Cassie shot him a horrified look. Jessie grinned back. "No, I don't think he's been peeing everywhere, but you know drunks. They reek like they haven't showered in a week or more."

"Nice imagery." Drew memories of the homeless littering the streets, from the one time they'd gone to the seedy part of Portland. Not pleasant – for those winos or for her family.

Jessie stepped into the room to peer over the couch. From his behavior, Cassie knew that's where he'd expected to find his dad. He frowned. "Not there." He walked around the room while Cassie waited at the entrance.

Raising her eyebrows at him, she asked, "Check the rest of the house out, I presume?"

"I guess."

Cassie had to laugh. He sounded like he'd been asked to ballet dance in front of the school. "Surely it's not that bad. I was here lots before, you know."

"Yeah, however that's when Todd was alive."

Cassie frowned, reminding herself that this was Jessie not Todd. "Did Todd do the cleaning? Was your dad always this bad?"

"The house was always messy, just nothing like this. I don't know what Todd did or didn't do. Just more of the information I'll never know. His room is clean though."

"Yeah, it always was."

She almost missed the curious look that crossed Jessie's face. "What?" She frowned as he studied her face. "I hung out there a lot. It's not like we could be around your dad. He was always drunk then, too."

Shaking his head, Jessie said, "My mom would never let me have a girl in my room. She'd be too worried we were doing things we shouldn't be."

"Well, that wasn't an issue with us. Inevitably, I ended up helping Todd pull his homework together." Cassie paused and pursed her lips. "On the other hand, my mother would freak if she'd found us in my bedroom."

"If...?"

"Of course we spent time in my room. Again, it wasn't like that with us." Cassie shrugged. "So upstairs to check the bedrooms or kitchen and backyard?"

"Kitchen first." He led the way.

The kitchen was a mess, maybe less of a mess than the living room, although Cassie wouldn't want to bet on that. She picked her way through the small room to the back door and opened it. The backyard was empty, too.

"Come on, let's check upstairs." Jessie ran up the stairs two at a time.

Cassie raced up behind him. Todd's door at the top of the stairs was closed. Jessie headed to his dad's room. Cassie looked inside curiously. This was cleaner than the rest of the house, though the smell was rank. Clothes littered the floor and the bed looked as though it hadn't changed in a year. She pinched her nostrils.

"He's not here, either." Jessie shook his head before turning back her way.

Cassie held up her hand. "Check the bathrooms and the closets."

He gave her a weird look, but did as she asked. "You don't think he'd have done something stupid, do you?"

"What's stupid? The man's an alcoholic who just lost his son. What happens if he can no longer drown his sorrows and find forgetfulness?"

Jessie's face thinned, his jaw firmed. Without a word he headed to Todd's bedroom, throwing the door open wide.

"Dad!" Jessie ran to the bed. Cassie ran up on the side.

Adam didn't look so good. His skin color was grayish and blotchy. From a drunk gone bad, or tears? She didn't know. She'd seen him sober and well turned out, and she'd seen him flat out drunk. Today he looked so much worse.

"Is he passed out?" Cassie hovered.

"Hell, if I know." There was a half empty bottle on the bed, and the smell of bourbon filled the small room.

Cassie watched as Jessie laid two fingers on his dad's neck to check for a pulse.

"He's alive and he's breathing."

"Sleeping off a binge?"

"I don't know. He doesn't look right."

"No, he doesn't. Try to wake him up." Cassie pulled out her phone as she watched Jessie shake his father. Adam's head wobbled with the movement, totally limp. "He's not asleep." As she cast an eye around the bed, she spotted a large bottle of sleeping pills and snatched it up.

It was empty.

***

Todd studied his father's pale face and shook his head. Now why would he do a stupid thing like that?

Cassie phoned for help and Jessie tried hitting his father – openhanded, to wake him up.

Todd, watching from the foot of the bed, wished he could have slapped his old man back to his senses a long time ago.

He watched Jessie's face as pain and horror swept away the anger, until his features settled into fear. His brother did care. If his father survived, maybe they could build something.

Adam needed to have a son around. He couldn't be trusted to do much on his own. Kind of like a big baby, still needing a nursemaid. His mother had filled that role until the drinking had become too much. Todd had grown into the role, only his dad had already been too far gone at that point.

Staring at his father, images in Todd's memory stirred. His father yelling at him and arguing. About what? Something stupid, knowing him. The two of them had some royal battles. Lately about his drinking and Todd's friends. Normal kid stuff.

Then... This one had been different.

Todd was driving and could hear yelling and screaming going on beside him. The vehicle had careened over the cliff. Todd's panicked attempts to...what? The frustrating memory eluded him. It just slipped away. Gone. Damn it. He stared down at his clenched fists. He was tired of this. So close and yet not quite there, in so many ways.

Sirens sounded in the distance, bringing Todd's attention back to the room. Cassie rushed out, then raced back in ahead of two men and a mess of equipment. The men dove at Adam and set about trying to save him. Todd watched before turning to speak with Cassie.

She was wrapped in Jessie's arms, her face buried against his chest. Cassie hadn't seen him. For the first time, she was more wrapped up in her world than his. His smile slipped. He knew that was the way it should be.

He understood something momentous was going on here. Some of his memories were filling in. When they did, he'd be able to leave. He knew that now.

The memory was that close, he could almost touch it. He hadn't wanted to leave his dad and Cassie.

Now it looked like Cassie would be just fine. Honestly, Todd was struggling a bit with that. Yet it did feel right.

But what about his dad?

CHAPTER EIGHTEEN

Deputy Magnusson walked into the liquor store at Belten Corner, the only liquor store close enough for Todd to have bought alcohol that night. He'd already called to find out when the same staff would be on duty. Luckily two were working now. Deciding it was time to put an end to this, he'd picked up and driven right over. Entering, he scanned the interior. Only a couple of shoppers browsed the aisles. He headed for the manager.

"Hi, Deputy Magnusson. Stephen Sanders, at your service." The two men shook hands. "I figured it would be better to give you my office. I'll bring the two men in here." He headed toward the door, tossing back, "I'll get Jim Benson first."

Gerome glanced around the small space – or rather the tiny space. There were, however, two chairs. He sat down in one and brought out his notebook, rummaging on the top of the desk for a pencil. A young, clean-cut male knocked on the doorframe.

"Deputy, I understand you have a couple of questions."

"Yes, Mr. Benson, please sit down. Did you work the evening shift two Friday's ago? It was May…"

"Doesn't matter what date it was. I always work on Fridays; so, yes."

Glancing up from his notebook, Gerome pursed his lips and nodded. "Good. We're looking to see if you remember Todd Spence, a young man who may have come in looking to buy alcohol."

"I know Todd. Man, is that what this is about? Am I in trouble? I probably should have handled it different, only Todd was my friend." He shrugged in defeat. "Yes, Todd was here. I can't sell to him because he's underage. He hasn't tried that in over a year. Only his dad was here, too, drunk and disorderly, as usual. I suppose, technically, Todd did buy the booze, his dad was too inebriated to get the money out or hand it over. Todd handled the transaction."

Gerome stared at him. "You're sure it was the boy's father?"

"Oh, yes. That man's been a hard burden for Todd. There's no mistaking him. I wouldn't normally serve him, only this was a matter of getting him out of the store with the least amount of trouble. I suppose I should have just refused to serve him, but I knew from experience how he'd react. He also wasn't driving, so it was easier to let them go."

"Did you see them get into the car?"

"Yes, I watched from the window." He shrugged. "Just to make sure Todd didn't have any trouble with his old man. With the promise of more booze, Adam went like a baby."

"Did you actually see them in the car? And saw them leave the parking lot?"

"Yes. Todd was driving and his father was in the passenger side."

Gerome sat back, stunned. Cassie had been right.

Todd Spence hadn't been alone.

***

Cassie watched the paramedics work on Adam, horrified at the invasiveness of the procedures and the sheer controlled chaos involved. Jessie squeezed her tight. They'd been shoved into the far corner of the room, out of the way. Arms wrapped around each other, they stood motionless.

Jessie had called his mother. She was en route to pick him up before both headed to the hospital behind the ambulance.

From the look of things, that should be soon. That Adam might have tried to commit suicide, shocked her. Yet she could see the decline. Like she'd mentioned to Jessie, his father probably hadn't been able to stop the pain after Todd's death. She could relate. Without having the special connection with Todd's spirit, she didn't know what she might have done herself.

"Okay, easy. Lift on the count of three."

Several people struggled to transfer the unconscious Adam onto a stretcher. Within minutes, he'd been strapped in and wheeled out of the room.

Cassie stared at the empty room, her arms dropping away as she took several steps toward the doorway. "Should we follow?"

"I will. You might as well go home."

She studied his pale almost blank face, as if not sure what to think anymore. First his brother, now his father. "Will he make it, Jessie?"

"What?" He blinked several times. "He might. I don't know how bad it is. They didn't say anything."

"No. It all happened so fast."

Cassie grabbed his hand, drawing him toward the hallway. "Come on. Your mom will be here soon."

"I'm fine." He wrapped his arm around her shoulders. "I'm shocked, scared, and, yes, horrified that he'd do this. However, I'm adjusting. Chances are he'll pull through. He's a tough old bastard."

"He's your father; be nice."

He glanced at her, a wry smile on his face. "Sorry, but it's the truth."

"Maybe, only right now he's in pain. And he had to have been hurting something awful to have done this."

"He couldn't handle Todd's death." Jessie opened the front door. "I don't quite know how I feel about that. It's a little hard to accept that he didn't want to live for the sake of his remaining son."

Cassie stopped on the front lawn. "Don't say that. He wasn't thinking clearly at all." She reached up to shake his shoulders. "He's only looking to stop the pain."

Jessie sighed. "I know, but it's hard. I hope he pulls through. I think he and I need time together."

"Sounds like a plan."

Cassie turned, hearing the sound of a vehicle. "Here's your mom. Go to the hospital. Your parents need you."

Jessie tugged her up into a close hug. "Thanks. I'm glad you were here."

She smiled up. "Me, too. I'm going home. Call when you know something."

Cassie waved good-bye as Jessie's mom drove up, her Honda Matrix spitting gravel as it screeched to a stop. His mother's face was distraught. It had to be tough to love a man bent on self-destruction.

Troubled, Cassie raced home.

***

Gerome pocketed his phone, thanking the store manager before heading for the hospital to check on Spence. Troubling facts needed to be pulled together. Adam Spence had some explaining to do. He might have been the last person to see his son alive. Now he'd possibly attempted suicide – Gerome wanted to know why. And decide if the two had anything to do with each other.

Mr. Spence was still in Emergency. According to the ER doctor he was still in danger. Gerome walked to the waiting room. Jessie sat holding an older woman's hands.

"Jessie. Good to see you."

Standing up, Jessie asked, "Deputy. Any news on my father? This is my mother. We haven't been able to find out anything."

Gerome acknowledged her and glanced back at the chaos going on behind him. "They're doing what they can for him."

He glanced at Sandra. "Ma'am, I hate to ask, but other than Todd's death, was there anything else going wrong in his world?"

Sandra's red-rimmed eyes stared in fear. "His world was falling apart. His drinking has gotten worse. He lost his job because of it, and I don't know what else. He probably doesn't either. Since Todd's accident...well, he's been drunk most of the time."

Gerome studied Jessie. "Jessie, I heard you and Cassie found him. I'm going to check out Mr. Spence's house in a moment. But did you see any note or some kind of message like a suicide note?"

Jessie stiffened. He opened his mouth, then closed it and shook his head. "No. But I honestly didn't look." He swallowed loudly. "Is it possible this was an accident?"

"Anything is possible." Gerome shoved his hands in his pockets, trying to formulate the questions that needed to be asked. "I need to ask you something else. Has Adam said anything about the night that Todd died?"

Jessie and Sandra exchanged looks.

Gerome continued. "Adam and Todd have been placed at the liquor store at Benton Square, close to quarter after eleven, just before the accident. They were together."

"Oh no," Sandra whispered. Her teary gaze locked on the chaos happening around her husband's bed. "You think he was there – in the car with Todd."

"I'm sorry to say, he was. Todd was driving and Adam was in the passenger seat as they left the parking lot."

Silence.

"So Todd was the driver?" Jessie asked.

"Unless they stopped somewhere and switched places?" Gerome nodded. "That isn't likely, although it's not impossible."

Jessie leaned forward, as if needing to know one more thing. "The person who saw them... Did they say whether Todd was drunk?"

Gerome smiled, grateful to have this answer. "Cassie was right. Todd didn't appear to have been drinking that night."

Relief washed over the young man's face. He might not have been close to his brother, still he obviously cared. "Thank you for that."

Sandra shook her head in confusion. "So what are you saying? That my son wasn't drinking and driving?"

"No, I don't think so. Todd was sober just after eleven and his accident was within minutes."

"So you were wrong?" Sandra sounded confused. Her face pinched as she took in the new information. "All this time, I thought he'd gone so far wrong that he was out drinking and carousing and getting into all sorts of trouble that night." She stood up, staring at him. "And instead of doing something wrong, he was actually helping his father?"

"That's possible. It would be good to speak with Adam. Maybe we could get a few answers."

Sandra crossed her arms over her chest, rocking slightly in place. Hope lit her eyes. "This might have been just a bad accident. Todd might have taken the corner too fast or overcorrected? He *was* a young driver. Could it have been so simple?"

"That is also possible."

Jessie continued to puzzle the mess over. "So where was my father? How did they meet? Did Todd have time to go home, pick him up and then go to the liquor store?"

Gerome sighed. He'd hope the young man might take a little longer to work this out. Kids were smart these days. "I can't say for sure until I speak with Adam. We know they were together when they left the store. How the accident happened, I can only surmise at. But, I think your father pulled Todd free afterwards, climbed up to the highway and called for help, using

Todd's cell phone. I think he either walked or hitched a ride back into town."

"And never said anything? Never stayed with Todd?" Shock and disgust filled the boy's voice.

"He was probably too drunk to really comprehend what had happened. And afterwards... Honestly? He probably didn't remember." Gerome motioned to forestall Jessie's next comment. "Before we continue speculating, we should give Adam a chance to explain."

"That won't be today." Dr. McIntosh came up behind them. "He's in critical condition and is being moved to the ICU."

Sandra covered her face with her hands, trying to halt her instinctive cry of pain. "May I see him?"

"Only for a few minutes now, because he's being moved. Once he's settled, you'll be able to see him again."

Jessie stood up and helped his mother to his father's bedside.

Gerome spoke quietly with the doctor. "Will he wake up soon?"

"No."

Gerome nodded. "In that case, I'll take my leave." With a final glance back, he headed to Adam Spence's house.

***

Cassie slowed her pace as she reached the corner of her block. She tilted her face to the sun and felt sheer joy at the warmth. At being alive and wanting to be alive. How much pain did it take before a person wanted to end it all? How ironic that Todd desperately wanted to live and his own father had been as desperate to die.

How sad.

What would she do if her father tried to commit suicide? It seemed so out of character, she couldn't imagine it. Or what about her mother? She was weaker. If she lost her husband, she might decide life wasn't worth living. As her daughter, Cassie would feel hurt, abandoned and even betrayed. Even now, just thinking about it all made her heart ache.

She might not be close to her parents, but she wouldn't want to be in Jessie's shoes right now. Her house came into sight. Pondering the quirks of life and death for those left behind, she realized Todd might not know what had happened.

Then again, he might have been the first to know.

Moodily, Cassie kicked a rock along the sidewalk at the front of her house. She reached for the doorknob.

"Cassie, is that you?"

"Yes, Mom." Cassie stepped inside.

"You're home late," her mother commented.

"Yeah. I got a little tied up."

"Oh, I was hoping you'd gone to see that nice Dr. Sanchez again."

"No. However I probably will need to tomorrow or the next day."

Abby walked through the living room, her face creased with concern. "Why? What happened?"

Cassie stood facing her mom and the words couldn't come. They refused to pass her lips. She tried again, only instead tears flooded her eyes and rolled down her cheeks. "Oh, Mom..."

Her mother rushed over. "Honey, what's the matter? You're scaring me. Tell me, please."

Cassie sniffled. "Adam Spence tried to commit suicide." At Abby's horrified gasp, she continued, "Jessie and I found him in Todd's room where he'd collapsed."

"Oh no, Cassie."

With a final sob, Cassie fell into her mother's arms.

***

Adam groaned, caught in a dense fog of horror and pain that wouldn't let him escape. Heavy white clouds pressed down tightly, squeezing his chest and face. His throat and stomach hurt. Everything ached.

His son's face shone before him. Todd. He smiled. Todd was fine, unhurt. His heart lightened. No father should see his son die before him and definitely not in front of him.

"Why did you leave me to die?"

Questions tormented Adam's dreams. His son's face wove through the dreams, his voice asking questions Adam couldn't answer.

Adam groaned again.

"Dad? Are you there? It's Jessie."

Jessie? His son. No, not his son – Sandra's son. His mind couldn't make sense of the names. Todd and Jessie. Jessie was Sandra's. Todd was his. Wasn't he? No, they were dead, weren't they? No. Todd was dead.

Pain swelled in his chest, building to a horrific weight, beyond bearing. It rose to a crescendo before bursting free. Tears poured.

"Adam, it's okay, honey. Don't cry, please."

He sobbed uncontrollably. As the floodgates opened, the pain slowly receded. He gasped for breath and opened his eyes. His beautiful wife sat on the side of his bed, holding his hand.

Why? Why hadn't she given up on him a long time ago? Worry marred her face. He tried to smile. "Hi."

"Adam," she cried out. "You're awake."

"Yes," he whispered as memories returned with his full consciousness. "But I wish I weren't." He rolled over, wanting nothing more than to fall back into forgetfulness.

"Please, don't say that," Sandra whispered. "Please, Adam. I love you. Please, don't do this. It's so hard now without Todd. I can't lose you, too."

"How will you feel about me, when you find out the truth?" he asked, rolling over to face her. His tormented gaze met her confused one. "I killed our son."

CHAPTER NINETEEN

The next day, Cassie strolled along the park edge, a coffee in her hand and Jessie on her mind. Todd had died in a terrible accident. His name had been cleared and the file closed.

Adam had been responsible. In a horrible, stupid way. Adam had called Todd while he was walking, drunk, to the liquor store. Todd had picked him up and taken him to the store. They'd argued on their way home. Adam had wanted to go back to the store to get a bottle he'd forgotten. Todd had just wanted to get his dad home.

Pissed, Adam had grabbed the steering wheel on the worst stretch of highway.

The accident had been inevitable at that point.

After the vehicle had finally stopped rolling, Adam had pulled Todd free, taken his cell phone to call someone – only he couldn't get through. Miraculously he wasn't injured. He'd climbed up the hill and had tried again. When that hadn't worked, he'd tossed the phone and had walked back to town. Somewhere along the way, the drunken fugue had taken over and he found his way home where he'd collapsed on his own couch. He had awakened to find cops pounding on his door to tell him his son had died in a bad car accident. The memories and reality had blended with every new bottle of liquor he poured down his throat, until he no longer knew where the truth started and his blurred memories began.

Only he couldn't forget the look on his son's face as he'd died in his arms.

Cassie found no comfort in being right.

Adam had been just trying to stop the pain. When the booze hadn't worked, he'd turned to pills.

"Yay, the swings are empty." She laughed and ran over to sit down on her favorite one. Looking around, she found Todd in front of her, grinning. Her smile turned melancholy. "Toddy bear."

He grinned, his smile so warm and loving, it brought tears to her eyes. "Hiya, kiddo."

"Hi." Did he know about his father? About all the things they'd been through? She opened her mouth to explain, knowing it would take a bit. "I need to tell you some things."

"It's okay. I already know." His eyes glowed with a wealth of knowledge. "It's time."

Cassie's words fell away as the pain and grief stepped up. Her bottom lip trembled. She'd known this time would come, only she'd hoped not so soon. "You're leaving?"

"Yes. Soon." His smile had an eerie illumination, as if lit from deep within. "I was there in my old bedroom. My dad will be okay. He needs time, but he can make it now." He paused. "I came to say good-bye to you."

Cassie's heart ached and her shoulders slumped. She nodded, whispering, "I understand."

"Do you? Because I'm not sure I do." He laughed. "This extra couple of weeks were special, Cassie. I'm so blessed to have known you. You are truly a light I take with me in my heart."

"That's such a nice thing to say." She smiled mistily. "And I feel the same about you. You lit up my life every single day."

"I know about Jessie, and you need to know, I approve. He's going through a tough time right now, but he's strong. He'll recover faster with you at his side."

Cassie laughed in delight, feeling his approval like a brush of warmth through her heart. She'd been so concerned that Todd would feel she'd replaced him. Or that Jessie would feel like he was a replacement. "You're very special, and I'm so blessed to have known you."

"Thank you." He stood up.

"Do you know the truth about your accident now?" Cassie couldn't resist asking. To make sure that he understood that, too.

"Yes."

Cassie closed her eyes in relief.

"As my father admitted what he'd done, my memories returned." He looked around. A huge glowing ray of sunlight shone on the park. He smiled and nodded toward it. "Now I'm at peace. I look back on this life and know how it has enriched my journey. It's okay. I'm no longer angry. I can leave now, knowing everything is as it should be."

He opened his arms and Cassie stepped into them. Immediately peace and love wrapped around her. Tears filled her eyes, then trickled past her tremulous smile. "Go in peace, Todd. You will be missed."

His wicked grin flashed. "Missed, but never forgotten, huh?"

Cassie laughed out of sheer joy. "Death might have changed your physical form, but not the Todd I know. Your spirit is still here."

"And I always will be. Live your life to the fullest, Cassie. Take each day as a gift and remember to live a little." He lifted a hand to her chin, and she felt his fingers stroke her cheeks like the kiss of butterfly wings. "And don't ever forget about me or that I loved you, baby. You were the one."

He dropped a tender kiss on her lips. Then he stepped back. "I have to go."

Tears ran in a steady stream down her cheeks. Cassie ignored them. She didn't want to miss one second of her last time with Todd. "Take care, Todd. Enjoy whatever comes next."

"I intend to." He waved a hand. "Love you, kiddo."

He turned and walked into the ray of sunshine. Cassie watched him glow, his whole body infused in light so bright it hurt her eyes.

Just like that he was gone.

She raced forward into the same sunshine. Just as she reached the spot, the sun went behind a cloud and the golden ray disappeared.

She sobbed once. Todd was gone. But instead of sadness, her heart swelled with poignant joy, even as tears raced down her cheeks. She spun around in circles, her arms wide open. He was where he belonged now, instead of being caught in a half existence wandering the earth alone.

She'd miss him. Always. But she was so happy for him, too.

Slowly, her energy running down, she retook her seat on the swing and picked up her forgotten coffee. Her heart was full of joy. She loved Todd and always would. He had a place in her heart forever.

Taking a sip of her drink, she looked around. Colors were brighter, the sunshine stronger. Life was truly a gift. Maybe death wasn't the horrible experience everyone believed it to be. She watched moms and kids walking across the grass, dogs bouncing alongside. At the old sandbox behind her, a young child was building a sandcastle.

Cassie smiled with pleasure. She heard her name and turned around.

Jessie waved at her from across the street; that special smile on his face was just for her. She waved back, watching him pick up the pace to the crosswalk. He'd be with her in a few minutes.

"Can you help me find my mommy?"

Cassie grinned down at the toddler staring up at her. "Of course I can. I'm sure she can't be far away." Cassie, her heart still full of exuberance, spun around looking for the missing parent. She searched the playground then out to the grassy fields. She frowned. There were no adults close by.

"Honey, what does your mommy look like?"

A child's laugh broke free. "Mommy's pretty."

Cassie grinned and turned back to smile at the cherub. "Is she?" Her smile fell away. The child was there, only the edges of the sandbox were visible behind her. Through her.

Shakes started to ripple down Cassie's spine. She closed the distance between them. The child laughed and her form slowly dissipated in front of Cassie. The sand in the box was flat and hard from years of being walked on. No sand sat heaped in the center as she thought she'd seen earlier.

Could she have been mistaken? Hearing a child's laughter, she glanced toward the hedge to see the same little girl running through the brush. *Through* the brush?

"Oh my," she whispered under her breath. The little girl was a giggling ghost. She laughed again, waved at Cassie and disappeared.

Standing stock still, Cassie finally understood a fundamental truth.

It's not that Todd *could* manifest in front of her, but that Cassie *could* see Todd. She, sixteen-year-old Cassie Merchant, owner of a boring average life in a boring average small town – could see ghosts.

"Cassie. Sorry I'm late." Jessie loped toward her across the grass.

With a last stunned look at the spot where she'd seen the child, Cassie turned and was instantly comforted by the warmth in Jessie's eyes. It didn't matter if she saw another spirit or a hundred spirits. She had Todd in her heart and Jessie in her life. Gorgeous Jessie, caring Jessie, special Jessie – her cohort in solving the mystery behind his brother's death and her friend all rolled up together. She laughed out loud for sheer joy.

Her life was complete.

Vampire in Denial

Blood doesn't just make her who she is...it also makes her what she is.

Like being a sixteen-year-old vampire isn't hard enough, Tessa's throwback human genes make her an outcast among her relatives. But try as she might, she can't get a handle on the vampire lifestyle and all the...blood.

Turning her back on the vamp world, she embraces the human teenage lifestyle--high school, peer pressure and finding a boyfriend. Jared manages to stir something in her blood. He's smart and fun and oh, so cute. But Tessa's dream of a having the perfect boyfriend turns into a nightmare when vampires attack the movie theatre and kidnap her date.

Once again, Tessa finds herself torn between the human world and the vampire one. Will blood own out? Can she make peace with who she is as well as what?

Or enjoy a different series!

Dangerous Designs

Drawing is her world...but when her new pencil comes alive, it's his world too.

Her...Storey Dalton is seventeen and now boyfriendless after being dumped via Facebook. Drawing is her escape. It's like as soon as she gets down one image, a dozen more are pressing in on her. Then she realizes her pictures are almost drawing themselves...or is it that her new pencil is alive?

Him...Eric Jordan is a new Ranger and the only son of the Councilman to his world. He's crossed the veil between dimensions to retrieve a lost stylus. But Storey is already experimenting with her new pencil and what her drawings can do - like open portals.

It ... The stylus is a soul-bound intelligence from Eric's dimension on Earth and uses Storey's unsuspecting mind to seek its way home, giving her an unbelievable power. She unwittingly opens a third dimension, one that held a dangerous predatory species banished from Eric's world centuries ago, releasing these animals into both dimensions.

Them... Once in Eric's homeland, Storey is blamed for the calamity sentenced to death. When she escapes, Eric is ordered to bring her back or face that same death penalty. With nothing to lose, can they work together across dimensions to save both their worlds?

About the author:

Dale Mayer is a prolific multi-published writer. She's best known for her Psychic Visions series. Besides her romantic suspense/thrillers, Dale also writes paranormal romance and crossover young adult books in several different genres. To go with her fiction, she also writes nonfiction in many different fields with books available on resume writing, companion gardening and the US mortgage system. She has recently published her Career Essentials Series. All her books are available in digital and print formats.

Books by Dale Mayer

Psychic Vision Series
Tuesday's Child
Hide'n Go Seek
Maddy's Floor
Garden of Sorrow
Knock, knock...

Death Series – romantic thriller
Touched by Death
Haunted by Death - (Fall 2013)

Novellas/short stories
It's a Dog's Life- romantic comedy
Sian's Solution – part of Family Blood Ties
Riana's Revenge – Fantasy short story

Second Chances…at Love
Second Chances - out now
Book 2 - Winter 2013/2014

Young Adult Books
In Cassie's Corner
Gem Stone (A Gemma Stone Mystery)

Design Series
Dangerous Designs
Deadly Designs
Darkest Designs

Family Blood Ties Series
Vampire in Denial
Vampire in Distress
Vampire in Design
Vampire In Deceit

Non-Fiction Books
Career Essentials: The Resume
Career Essentials: The Cover Letter
Career Essentials: The Interview
Career Essentials: 3 in 1

Connect with Dale Mayer Online:
Dale's Website – www.dalemayer.com
Twitter – http://twitter.com/#!/DaleMayer
Facebook – http://www.facebook.com/DaleMayer.author

Printed in Great Britain
by Amazon